The Rt. Hon Sir Geoffrey Pattie gained a degree in Law from St. Catharine's College, Cambridge. Deciding against the pursuit of a career at the Bar, Geoffrey went into the less staid world of advertising where he became the managing director of one of leading agencies of the early 1960s, CDP.

Geoffrey Pattie became the MP for Chertsey and Walton in 1974 and served the constituency for 23 years until his retirement from the House of Commons at the election of 1997. He served in Margaret Thatcher's Governments first as a Defence Minister from 1979 to 1984, a period which covered the Falklands War of 1982. He became Minister for Information Technology in the Department of Trade and Industry from 1984 to 1987. He was also Vice Chairman of the Conservative Party in charge of International Relations from 1990 to 1997.

While still an MP Geoffrey Pattie became Chairman of GEC Marconi the defence manufacturer and on his retirement from the House he went to work full-time at the company first as Director of Marketing and subsequently as Director of Communications.

He now runs Terrington Management, a consulting partnership in Westminster.

Geoffrey Pattie was knighted in 1987 and made a member of the Privy Council in 1986. He is Deputy Colonel Commandant of the Royal Green Jackets (TA and Cadets).

One of Our Delegations is Missing

Geoffrey Pattie

Manor House Publishing

First published 2002
©2002 by Geoffrey Pattie

Manor House Publishing, 45 Great Peter Street, London SW1P 3LT

Cataloguing in Publication Data
A catalogue record for this title is available from the British Library

ISBN 0 9542136 0 2

Printed and bound in Britain by Biddles

1

Every Picture Tells a Story

♦

THE GOVERNOR, in white full ceremonial dress together with plumed cocked hat, looked surprised as Rosie, in the very act of shaking his hand, bent her head forward and covered his shoes and shins with the partially digested remnants of the airline lunch.

In his entire obscure career in the recesses of the Foreign Office, the Governor had never met a Member of the Mother of Parliaments until this moment. As far as he knew this was the standard form of greeting given by MPs on arrival abroad. He wriggled his toes uneasily in the vomit-laden shoes as more members of the parliamentary delegation descended the steps of the small commuter aircraft and made towards him. The Governor's manservant, Kelp, sank to the occasion by grabbing a fire bucket and swishing the offending particles from the shoes of Her Britannic Majesty's representative, at the same time putting an inch of water in each of them. Kelp would have to go.

None of the other members of the party were sick on the Governor, although some of them looked pale. There were five of them altogether, two Labour, two Conservative and a Liberal Peer called Lord Hogshead. The other Labour Member with Rosie Long was Albert Blackhead from a Yorkshire mining seat. He always wore a trilby hat and was first in line for all foreign visits. His voting record when in London was so wayward that his Whips were glad to see him abroad on the basis that at least they knew where he was.

Mrs Rosie Long had represented a Newcastle seat for thirty two years and she was respected as a highly redoubtable campaigner. She had lost her seat on Labour's National Executive Committee the previous year, but this had been mainly due to factional in-fighting and horse-trading of votes. Her peroxide hair surmounted a square, determined face, onto which make-up now had to be applied like mortar.

The two Tories were Sir Wentworth Stringer, a former wartime commando and now a distinguished-looking backbencher, and Rollo Herbert-Fitzherbert, a self-appointed and self-opinionated expert on Pacific affairs, who had a penchant for duty-free liquor. He was once reported to have sat down on an airport tarmac and kicked until he was allowed his duty-free booze. He was Chairman of the Friends of the Faraway Islands, although the good people of the Faraway Islands neither knew nor cared if they had any friends anywhere. Events were shortly going to change their attitude.

Lord Hogshead had a family knowledge of the wine trade and on that account he had no reason whatever to visit the South Pacific, where no wine was to be seen. He lived in hope, however, (and he was rarely disappointed) that new local drinks would be offered so that he could extend his repertoire.

When everyone had greeted the Governor, Kelp brought round the Governor's official conveyance, a former London taxi. Rosie Long was amused to see this and set off at a brisk trot to get aboard, the Governor squelching alongside. The rest of the party were fitted into other cars and soon the small convoy was leaving the airfield and setting course for Port Roger, the capital of the Faraway Islands, about three miles away.

As Rosie looked out of the window she recalled the main features of the Foreign Office brief about the Faraway Islands. The islands were discovered by Captain Cook and were later settled by the Dutch, from whom the British took them in the 1820s. Since then a largely British population had built up, often boosted by significant shipwrecks. The original settlers in the 1830s were mainly Scottish sheep farmers and they brought some of their sheep with them. The sheep flourished on the western, and more exposed, of the two main islands, Makeaway Island. The eastern island, Takeaway, was more overgrown and had given itself to a certain amount of fruit farming, as the soil was good for growing and the climate was kind. There were very few roads and the total population hardly exceeded one thousand.

The Governor, Mr Cunningham, lived in the Official

Residence on the edge of the capital, Port Roger, on the way in from the airfield. Dusk is a rather brief phase in the south Pacific and Rosie Long had not realised that it was nearly nightfall when they landed. She was not therefore able to see very much from the taxi's windows, apart from a lot of fruit trees, before Kelp swung the wheel and the taxi turned into Government House.

The title Government House, or Official Residence of the Governor, conveys a picture out of keeping with the reality of Port Roger. A modest country rectory of quite pleasing proportions stood ready to welcome the visitors and issuing from the front door came Mrs Cunningham, small and forceful. Her forced joviality, however, rather betrayed an anxiety. It was some years since any MPs had found their way to the islands.

The party gathered in the hall as the luggage was piled in behind them, threatening to hem them in completely. The Governor saved the situation by proclaiming, 'Let's all have a drink,' and led the way into the drawing room.

Lord Hogshead had a fresh gleam in his eye as Kelp went round the room soliciting requests for drinks and producing an approximate response.

'I'm afraid we only get four boats a year from England nowadays, so we may not have what you would prefer. No Newcastle Brown Ale, I'm afraid, Mrs Long,' said the Governor, trying to be cheerful and still remembering his feet.

'I'd like a Martini, please,' said Mrs Long slightly tartly. She hated being typecast. Kelp fumbled among the bottles until he found one marked *Martini* and poured out what was in it. Hogshead intercepted the glass and sipped it. 'That's water,' he said, handing it back to Kelp, adding quietly, 'She won't know the difference.'

'Well,' said the Governor when everyone had a drink, 'Welcome to the Faraway Islands.' They raised their glasses. As they did so, Kelp re-entered the room and went straight to the chair in which the Governor was sitting. Without a word he dropped on one knee and seized the Governor's left shoe, which he proceeded to pull off. He emptied the water out of it with a splash in the grate and repeated the performance with the other shoe. He then removed each of the Governor's socks in turn and left the room with them. The Governor tapped his bare right foot on the carpet quite cheerfully, aware that Kelp's behaviour had caught the attention of the room.

'First class people, the islanders,' said the Governor. 'Plenty of initiative. Do things for themselves. Rather like Britain around 1900.'

'Sounds ideal,' sighed Sir Wentworth, who wished Britain was still like Britain in 1900.

Mrs Long was not amused. 'Being in the Britain of 1900 means that virtually every man and woman here works for the Faraway Islands Company. True or false, Governor?'

'True enough, Mrs Long, although they hardly feel exploited.'

'I didn't say they are exploited. You have been reading my script,' she added, with a rare flash of humour. 'Anyway, tell us about the politics.'

The Governor settled himself back in his armchair and drummed his bare feet on the carpet.

'There are, of course, no politics in the sense that we would understand the term in the Islands. There is an Executive Council, half elected and half appointed by me, and two of its members are coming to meet you tomorrow and to accompany you on the visits we have planned for you. You will be aware of the Scott Report of five years ago which recommended major investment in the Islands because of the strategic situation and because of the presumed existence of valuable raw materials such as oil. So far ...' the Governor coughed politely, 'successive governments have not yet implemented these recommendations.' Governors were always on safe ground when they could speak of successive governments.

'In terms of external politics,' continued the Governor, 'there is a claim to the sovereignty of the Islands by the Republic of Marranesia, which as you will know is 400 miles away from here and bases its claim as the successor government to the Dutch who once were in occupation. We have in recent years extended our contacts with Marranesia, which is now a Marxist republic and, indeed, our air contact is entirely by way of that country.'

'What is the likelihood of Marranesia using force?' asked Herbert-Fitzherbert.

'Remote in the extreme,' replied the Governor. 'I have recently paid a courtesy visit to the Military Governor of Puna Mes, the nearest Province to us, and he couldn't have been nicer. They have to maintain their claim to keep their population happy, but they told me not to expect them to take it seriously. I told them that we did not take their threat seriously. In fact, we rely entirely on a contingent of Royal Marines to act as a deterrent. They have modernised their armed forces, which they use largely to keep internal order. Most western nations, including Britain, have sold the Marranesians modern weapon systems of varying types.'

Everyone seemed satisfied with the Governor's exposition and so, in the absence of any further questions, the Governor suggested that they might like to see their rooms and prepare for dinner. Mrs Long was keen to restore her physical equilibrium, so she excused herself from dinner, which suited the rest of the party as they could revert to the stag status which was the state in which parliamentary delegations felt most at ease.

On the following morning the two members of the Executive Council, Mr Frond and Mr Mulch, arrived at Government House to discuss the visit programme. Although the population of the Islands was small, not to say tiny, the overall area was roughly equivalent to Wales. Travel was possible mainly by light aircraft to remote grass strips or by boat along the coast for shorter journeys.

The delegation divided into two groups, lots having been drawn, the losers having to accompany Mrs Long. Mrs Long and Sir Wentworth (ever a graceful loser) set off to talk to schoolchildren on various parts of the Islands, and the second group, bolstered by the presence of Lord Hogshead, was scheduled to visit some examples of island industry such as fishing and the use of fish products and the hand-carving of wood. These latter products would have been naturals for the tourist industry had there been one, but the continuous studied neglect of the Islands by British governments meant that these opportunities were seldom, if ever, exploited. It would only be fair, however, to make it clear that opinion on the Islands in favour of 'progress' was by no means unanimous. Executive Council member John Mulch had described progress as a two-edged spoon.

The British parliamentarians were assiduous in performing their investigative tasks on the Faraway Islands and they had little difficulty in filling out their seven days with visits and presentations and touring. Throughout this time the Governor and Mrs Cunningham provided the focal point for the dinner parties and cocktail parties attended by what Whitehall would describe as the great and the good of the Islands.

In due course the delegation found themselves packing on their last morning at Port Roger. There was to be a formal luncheon to commemorate the event and at the lunch, during the course of their respective speeches, the Governor presented Mrs Long with a penguin beak in the shape of an astray and she in turn presented the Governor with a set of House of Commons Wedgwood ashtrays and boxes in pastel shades of blue and green. Toasts were drunk in Californian wine, which had been presented by a passing US Navy destroyer the previous year. The menu proclaimed several island delicacies, such as penguin feet soup and breast of penguin, and the star liqueur was a liquid apparently distilled from seaweed. Everyone tried at least a sip, with only Lord Hogshead returning to the glass a second time.

Suitably warmed with this memorable fare, the delegation was driven to the Port Roger airfield where the island brass band was in position, ready to discharge its limited repertoire. Hands were shaken, the Governor's plumes fluttered in the constant wind, and the band played *Rule Britannia*. The aircraft taxied and took off and soon Takeaway Island was a carpet of green below them.

Rosie Long settled down with her papers to make some notes, but soon the stewardess was patrolling the aisle to ensure all seat belts were securely fastened because there was turbulence ahead. The airline was operating an SD 330 made by Shorts of Belfast and, although an excellent aircraft, it was unpressurised and had therefore to fly directly into much of the cloud.

The storm was rather violent, even the aircrew agreed about that. The aircraft bucked up and down and from side to side. Periodically it sank like a stone, leaving the passengers' stomachs at their original height. Rosie Long knew she was going to have to make a spectacle of herself again. This time she knew she was going to be really ill. She could feel the idea of nausea gaining ground in her mind. It was as though she had been chained to her seat and made to watch the last ten telerecordings of Tory Party Conference.

On the flight deck the problems were different. A light

indicated a possible engine malfunction, but it was always possible that the fault was merely electrical in the control panel, causing the light to come on when it had no reason to. On the other hand, if the light was genuine — and there was no means of checking it during flight — then the aircraft was in trouble. The Captain decided that as they were not yet half way, they would have to turn back to Port Roger.

The news of the unscheduled return was announced and evinced no audible response. To the suffering passengers a landing anywhere, even in Hell itself, would have been welcomed. The storm showed no sign of abating and the light indicating an engine fault remained firmly on as the plane reappeared over Port Roger airfield.

As the plane landed, it pulled up sharply and turned to one side of the 4,000-foot runway. As it did so, Sir Wentworth Stringer saw a C130 Hercules aircraft bearing markings which he did not recognise.

Around it was standing a group of military personnel in olive green uniforms. The Hercules had not been there when they took off nearly an hour ago.

The aircraft taxied towards the main reception building and then stopped. The Captain came onto the intercom. 'I have been told by the control tower that in the last half hour the Faraway Islands have been invaded by Marranesian forces who have annexed the Islands. All resistance has ceased and the Governor has surrendered. You will be met by the Commander-in-Chief of the Marranesian Forces, General Hernando.'

'I wonder where that wretched Governor fellow is now,' said Stringer angrily.

'Away eating his cocked hat, I should think,' offered Lord Hogshead.

'The band can forget about *Rule Britannia,*' added Herbert-Fitzherbert.

'Well, here we are again,' said Albert Blackhead, who was good at stating the obvious. Indeed they were there again, only this time they were greeted by a General in an olive green uniform who saluted smartly as the rather dishevelled group came down the steps, led by the exceedingly dishevelled Rosie Long.

Rosie was overcome both by the glorious presence of Marxist

troops and by travel sickness. In attempting to salute the former, she only succeeded in succumbing to the latter. Her arms, which were intended to grasp the General in a comradely fashion around his shoulders, instead flapped feebly in the area of his elbows as she sank to the ground and was violently ill on his ankles.

As she grasped his ankles and shins for some modicum of support in her moment of need, the press camera bulbs flashed and an unforgettable picture — soon to appear above the caption *British MP kisses the feet of Marranesian Conqueror* — had been taken. The humiliation of Great Britain was complete.

2

Lord Mafeking
Takes Charge

♦

FOR A FEW DAYS BEFORE ROSIE LONG'S photograph hit the world's
press, something approaching a sense of alarm had begun to settle
on the Foreign Office and the Ministry of Defence in London. In
Gazebo, the capital of Marranesia, the British Ambassador was
sending a stream of telegrams to London each day reporting the
strident anti-British tone of the government-controlled press and
the detailed statements of the Marranesian claim to the Faraway
Islands on the government-controlled television and radio.

When the Marranesians mobilised their reserves and sent their
regular forces on full-scale manoeuvres, then — and only then
— did the Foreign Office force itself to believe that something
along the lines of an invasion could be about to happen to the
British Faraway Islands.

For years the Foreign Office had persuaded a succession of
well-meaning Foreign Secretaries that Britain had to rid itself of
the Faraway Islands and as many other relics of colonialism as
possible. In recent years negotiations had been held in New York,
but the Faraway inhabitants had remained steadfastly
unimpressed and equally steadfastly British. It was still possible
to buy mint condition George VI Coronation mugs in the general
store in Port Roger.

In recent months anyone with half an eye on the Marranesian
scene and an ounce of grasp of human nature would have known
that the Marxist military dictatorship was looking for a suitable
foreign venture to deflect attention from its serious economic
and political problems at home — anyone, that is, except those
whose job it was to observe.

There were some who claimed in later months that the decision
some months previously by the Ministry of Defence to pension

off the Faraway Islands patrol ship HMS *Reluctance* had been another contributory factor which encouraged the Marranesians to believe that Britain would accept an invasion as a *fait accompli.* In the smoking room of the House of Commons, however, there was no doubt that the Foreign Office were following directly in the Burgess, Maclean and Philby line by betraying British interests.

On the sixth floor of the Ministry of Defence there was a realisation that the seventy valiant Royal Marines on the Faraways would not be able to withstand a full-scale assault by the Marranesians. Various plans were being hastily examined from the filing cabinet marked *Contingencies,* but as no-one had ever given the invasion of the Faraways a high possibility rating, no precise plan existed and the nearest plan was based on the Walchesan Expedition of 1797, with certain revisions to take account of new technology. It was well understood in MOD that much would depend on the incisive brain and decisive personality of the Secretary of State for Defence himself.

Lord Mafeking, the Secretary of State for Defence, stared gloomily round the light ochre walls of his large office. His main problem was how to find out exactly where the Faraway Islands were without having to ask Brian or Jolyon, his irritatingly intelligent Private Secretaries. He got up from the oval table which he habitually used as a desk and walked over to the large globe which was suspended in a polished frame and correctly angled 23° degrees off the vertical. He had given up geography (and most other subjects) at Eton and he rather regretted it, particularly when Cabinet discussions turned to countries about which he would like to have known more — countries like Russia and America.

Lord Mafeking was a tall man, well over six feet in height, with thinning dark hair and a large round face. The eyes were somewhat too close together, the nose large and slightly bulbous, the mouth full and friendly, the complexion pink and the ears on the big side. He had a hearing aid which everyone knew about and on this day he was wearing a dark green tweed suit and, insensitively in modern Tory circles, an old Etonian tie. On account of his hearing problem, he was often too loud in speech.

Lord Mafeking twirled the globe gently, half hoping that the

Faraway Islands would give off some form of incandescence and put him out of his discomfiture. Once he thought he had found them but 'they' turned out to be the Cocos and Keeling Islands. Where the hell were they?

He squatted on his haunches and rotated the globe. As New Zealand passed for the fourth time he was sure he had seen the Faraways. He put out his right hand to stop the world but in doing so he overbalanced and fell over on his right side. A despairing attempt to halt his downward progress only succeeded in an unavailing clutch at the frame which supported the globe, with the result that the frame and globe toppled over and fell onto the now recumbent Lord Mafeking. His Lordship had instinctively protected his head with his arm as the globe descended but his hearing aid was dislodged from its customary perch in his left ear. He therefore did not hear the approach of Brian and Jolyon from the Private Office until their suede-clad feet appeared in his line of vision.

'Secretary of State, are you all right?' asked Brian, trying to see signs of life from under the globe.

'You seem to be carrying the whole world today, Secretary of State,' quipped Jolyon tastelessly.

'Shut up, Jolyon, and help the Secretary of State up,' said Brian, who was the Principal Private Secretary and was very conscious of his position. Jolyon was but the Assistant Private Secretary. Both of them harboured ambitions to be Permanent Secretary in about twenty years, by which time the glacier-like movement of the Civil Service machine would have spewed them out as candidates for the top job. A tour in a Private Office was an indicator that a young civil servant was regarded as being in the fast stream. After such a tour he could expect to disappear from the glamour of the sixth floor and go to a remote MOD site.

The main aim in life for the Private Office was to keep their noses clean and, if at all possible, to avoid actually losing their Secretary of State. In Lord Mafeking's case this was by no means a remote possibility. Lord Mafeking had, for example, great difficulty in remembering his MOD official pass which he had to insert in the machine at the south door when he arrived each day. He had even greater difficulty remembering the number that he had to punch into the machine in order to make the turnstile admit him. Thus it was that Jolyon met him each time he arrived, gave him his card plus a postcard with his special number on it. Armed with these, Lord Mafeking passed through the turnstile each day and Britain's defences were secure.

Brian and Jolyon knew perfectly well that Lord Mafeking's sudden interest in the world sprang from a desire to learn the precise location of the Faraway Islands, but that he was loath to display his appalling ignorance by having to ask them. They helped him to his feet and put the world back in its place.

'Thank you,' he roared and Jolyon at once dropped to his hands and knees on the carpet and looked for the hearing aid. He found it and handed it back. Communication with Lord Mafeking without his hearing aid was intermittent.

'Secretary of State, there is a brief here for you on the Faraway Islands. I thought you might like to glance at it before CDS comes to see you,' said Brian.

'When is that?' asked Lord Mafeking slightly grumpily because he was aware that he was being manipulated.

'He's actually outside now, Secretary of State.'

'So my opportunity for "in depth evaluation" will be somewhat limited.' Lord Mafeking could be quite sarcastic when he tried. Brian and Jolyon smiled and Lord Mafeking walked over to his table and picked up the brief. There on the first page was a map of the Pacific, showing the position of the Faraway Islands and their close proximity to Marranesia. There followed some pages of background data about the islands and the Marranesian armed forces. Lord Mafeking asked Brian to show in the Chief of the Defence Staff.

It was the Navy's turn to fill the top spot in Britain's armed forces and Admiral Sir Trimmer Halliard was acknowledged as among the most valiant of the current Whitehall warriors. He had been mentioned in memoranda for sterling forays against the Foreign Office and the Treasury and had also distinguished himself in a full-scale row with the Department of Trade covering the cost of the hydrographic survey vessel. Admiral Halliard had not, as it happened, been involved in any action at sea, which put him in an excellent position as the Prime Minister's principal defence adviser because nothing he was going to say could possibly be cluttered or obscured by the subjective irrelevance of personal experience.

Lord Mafeking's office was arranged so that he could have meetings around the polished oval table, as he could be less formal and sit on the squashy ochre armchair and sofa laid out in a square close to the door. Lord Mafeking decided to remain at the table because CDS invariably brought a toy model with him which he liked to slide around the table.

True to form, the Admiral produced from his pocket a model of a nuclear submarine and placed it on the table in front of him.

'Nuclear submarine, Secretary of State.'

Lord Mafeking stared at the model in silence. He had heard of nuclear submarines and he had even been on board one. He had also gradually got used to the Admiral's style of speech in the twelve months since the Prime Minister's call to his fishing retreat had brought him, still in his wellingtons, hotfoot to London and into office as Secretary of State for Defence. The Admiral was showing signs of commencing his dissertation for advanced four year olds. Lord Mafeking nodded.

'Got to decide what to do. Faraway Islands. Situation grim. Need a naval presence. ASAP. Nuclear sub — very fast — keeps underwater — get there soon.'

'What does it do when it gets there?' asked Lord Mafeking suddenly.

'Goes on patrol.'

'To do what?'

'Hunt the enemy.'

'What does it do when it finds the enemy.'

'You decide, Secretary of State. You decide.'

With more than a trace of self-satisfaction, the Admiral pushed the nuclear sub across the table to Lord Mafeking.

'How long will it take to get there?' asked Lord Mafeking, pushing the model back across the table to the Admiral.

'About three weeks.'

'Where is the nearest one now?'

'Thousands of miles from the Faraways. HMS *Relapse* is at Gibraltar. She'd do. Your decision, Secretary of State.' So saying, the Admiral returned the nuclear sub back across the table.

'How big is the Marranesian Navy?' asked Lord Mafeking.

'Two World War Two cruisers, a pre-war aircraft carrier and some newer ships, some of them bought from us.'

The Admiral had obviously anticipated this question because he had with him the latest edition of Jane's Fighting Ships and this he proceeded to open at the Marranesian entry and show the various photographs.

'How soon do you want a decision?' asked Lord Mafeking, pushing the model back to the Admiral.

'Today. Should have been three weeks ago. Shouldn't have believed Foreign Office fellows. Your decision, Secretary of State.' Once more the much-travelled model slid over the polished table.

Detecting the danger of an imminent decision, Brian spoke. 'You might wish to refer this to the Prime Minister before finally deciding, Secretary of State,' said Brian nervously. He did not dare to move the model.

Lord Mafeking thought for a moment, but only a moment. Thinking for him was rarely a lengthy process.

'I can tell the Prime Minister later. At this stage this need be no more than the sort of manoeuvre that's within the Ministry of Defence's purview. Let's do it. Despatch HMS *Collapse.*'

'*Relapse.*'

'Whatever it's called. Anything else?'

'No thank you, Secretary of State.'

The Admiral stood up, pocketed his model and headed for the door.

'Oh, CDS,' called Lord Mafeking. 'You'd better be getting an armada ready, don't you think?'

This was one of those semi-requests which could be left as a metaphorical aside if subsequent events showed it to have been wrong, or made out to be a positive request if shown to have been necessary with the wisdom of hindsight. CDS departed for his office next door, leaving Lord Mafeking wondering how he would ever be able to generate that timid degree of informality that came from habitual use of first names. Lord Mafeking knew that CDS had a first name other than Trimmer. Babies just weren't christened Trimmer. Above all, Lord Mafeking rather hoped to be called Arthur by his principal adviser, but it had never happened.

Brian went to his desk in the outer office to complete his notes of the meeting and to wonder where Lord Mafeking had come across the word *purview*, which he had never heard him use before.

Lord Mafeking decided that there was time for a crap before his next meeting, so he went over to the bathroom in the far corner of his office. His Private Secretaries felt that they had to be aware of this particular manoeuvre, otherwise they were fruitlessly engaged trying to make contact on the telephone or putting their heads round the door only to find the room empty. With the approval of the Permanent Secretary (without which nothing was able to happen) a device had been placed under the bathroom step and this device triggered a buzzer on the Private Secretaries' desks, thereby telling them that their Lord and Master was relieving himself. The mean average for the shorter call of nature was twenty-six seconds, with Jolyon holding the record with eleven correct time guesses out of a possible eighteen in one week. If the buzzer did not sound after about twenty-five to thirty seconds, it indicated to the young men that the Lord had settled down for the longer call of nature.

A telephone had been installed in the bathroom of the sort of which any self-respecting Hilton or Intercontinental Hotel would be proud. Brian and Jolyon had never had to use the loo extension until this very morning when Brian had to interrupt the Lord's thinking.

'It's the Prime Minister, Secretary of State. The Prime Minister can't wait.'

'Nor can I,' came the irritated reply, so the Prime Minister was put through. Lord Mafeking settled himself on the seat.

'Good morning, Prime Minister. Yes, I have heard about the problems at the Faraway Islands. Yes, we are doing something about it. I have authorised one of our nuclear submarines to move. I thought you'd like that. About three weeks. No, we can't get it there any faster. Yes, we are looking at plans for a Task Force. There's going to be a statement in the House tomorrow by the Foreign Secretary. I see. Very well. Why does my office echo so? It's probably because I'm sitting on, er.. the window ledge. No, I won't jump out. Yes, it would look bad, I agree. No, I don't want to make things worse than they already are. I'll have a statement drafted for you to see in the morning. Later tonight? Oh, very well. Yes. Yes. Certainly, Prime Minister. Goodbye.'

Not the best place to have a conversation with one's boss, thought Lord Mafeking as he concluded operations, unwittingly sounded the all clear buzzer and found himself surrounded by Brian and Jolyon.

'I have asked the Head of DS11 to draft a statement for you, Secretary of State. It will cover proposed movement by our own forces and will lay much of the blame for our lack of readiness on the Labour Party.'

'But we have been in office for three years,' replied Lord Mafeking. Even he could spot a political non-starter.

'True, Secretary of State, but DS11 in their draft will point to a prolonged period of unpreparedness which has led to the present crisis, in so many words. It would not be necessary to apportion blame directly, but the meaning could be implied.'

Lord Mafeking felt that it would be unlikely if the distaste he felt for these young men could possibly diminish during his period in office. They and the Heads of the various Defence Secretariat branches were so assured and so brilliant with words that he could well believe them capable of certainly anything provided their promotion depended on it. On the other hand, however much he distrusted their brilliance and felt uneasy with them, he had to rely totally on them. They would prepare a draft paper with background speaking notes attached.

It was nearly lunchtime and Lord Mafeking had agreed to lunch with his old friend Johnnie Mollusc, the Leader of the House of Lords. He agreed that a draft statement should be prepared by early evening and then asked the Private Office to have his car brought round to the south door.

Once through the turnstiles of the south door, he was out on the steps of the Ministry of Defence building and was ready to be swept up by his driver, Staff Sergeant Banger. The Staff Sergeant had a warm and friendly exterior, behind which lay a shrewd brain and a good eye to the main chance. As driving jobs go, this job with the Secretary of State was a good one. The parliamentary recesses were long and Lord Mafeking tended to go off to the country and only have official boxes sent to him by train. At such times Sergeant Banger would draw on his qualification as a London cabby — he having passed the necessary knowledge tests — and in this way he would boost the Banger family income several-fold. In addition, he actually rather liked the job. As his man was very often the guest of honour at the various functions, he would take on the reflected aura and find the premier position reserved for his parking, or good food for him at the drivers' door. He liked the special white oval disc that allowed him to drive through Horse Guards and out into Whitehall at any time, provided he was carrying his boss in the car. Driving into Buckingham Palace and Chequers was his idea of something slightly out of the ordinary. He also had something of a sneaking liking for Lord Mafeking. To him the Secretary of State was an amiable old buffer who seemed to want to talk in the privacy of the car about his problems.

Lord Mafeking chattered away about the morning's events as Sergeant Banger drove him towards St James's. Lord Mafeking seemed curiously able to relax with Sergeant Banger, far easier, for example, than trying to relax and explain anything to Lady Mafeking.

Half way up St James's, Banger stopped the car and Lord Mafeking got out at his club. Inside he was greeted by Lord Mollusc and found himself the centre of attraction at the bar with everyone plying him with questions about the Faraway Islands and the state of our military preparedness. To such latter questions Lord Mafeking would simply say that careless talk costs lives and allow himself to be taken off to the dining room.

After the Polynesian waitress informed that that 'watercless soup was off', they consumed steak and kidney pudding and the club claret, followed by the execrable club coffee, in deep armchairs in the smoking room.

'This is going to be a very difficult business, Arthur,' said Johnnie Mollusc, when he was satisfied they were out of earshot.

'And I don't just mean militarily, I mean politically. It will be bad enough in our House, but in the Commons there will be a hell of a storm if the invasion takes place. It is going to, isn't it?'

Arthur Mafeking nodded. 'Probably tomorrow,' he said. 'I agree with you, Johnnie. PM will take a strong line. Don't know about the rest of the Cabinet.'

'The rest of the Cabinet won't get a look-in. You mark my words. We'll be straight back to the kitchen cabinet of a few years ago.'

Johnnie Mollusc was a wise old owl and he was usually right, especially on House of Lords matters. As Leader of the Lords he had the permanent problem of ensuring a government majority when so many even of those Peers who took the Tory whip seemed to put other interests first and the turnout rose and fell alarmingly. Patronage was not the carrot to their Lordships that it was to their brethren in the 'other place', as the Commons was known.

Sergeant Banger was at the kerb, ready to convey Lord Mafeking away in the black Ministry of Defence Granada. Back at the Ministry, the afternoon was spent on a series of meetings on subjects, all of which were about to be subsumed under the Faraways, and those involved knew it. It was, however, an opportunity for these people both civil servants and military men, to take the Secretary of State's mind on these matters.

Late in the afternoon Brian came in with the draft statement and its author, a nervous fellow called Hollow. Lord Mafeking read it carefully and arranged to meet Brian later in the evening in his room at the House of Lords after the opera. Last minute amendments could still be made then to enable the draft to be got over to Number Ten in time for the PM's late box.

Lord Mafeking was then taken to meet Lady Mafeking, who had been brought up from Eltham by Sergeant Banger. The Mafekings lived at Eltham in an old rectory which they had agreed to in a hurry on the telephone, believing it to be near the airport because Lord Mafeking's hearing aid batteries had been on low power and he thought the estate agent said Feltham — not Eltham. But, nothing daunted, they had buckled down in true old-fashioned British fashion and made something of an otherwise unpromising situation.

Lady Mafeking had a shrill voice, which unnerved most people on first meeting. She had a keen interest in music, hence the evenings at the opera where they would be the guests of Lord Silicon, Chairman of one of the major electronic companies. On these occasions, Lord Mafeking preferred to slip out of his hearing aid and stare out at the audience from the depth of the Silicon box. He believed the opera to be *Aida*, but even the arrival of an assortment of camels and horses failed to arouse his interest. His military thoughts were well beyond the contents of the Grand March.

During the second interval he went into Bow Street outside the Opera House, found Sergeant Banger, and got into the car. He had excused himself from Lord Silicon on grounds of urgent government business, which happened for once to be true.

'About that statement tomorrow, Me Lord,' said Sergeant Banger. He preferred to give that style of greeting as it sounded rather good and it was shorter than saying 'Secretary of State'.

'What about it?' replied Lord Mafeking.

'I think the Foreign Office are out to stitch you up.'

'What does that mean — "stitch me up"?'

'It means make it look like you're to blame, Me Lord,' said Sergeant Banger patiently. He wondered at times how his Lordship had got so far in the world with so many gaps in his education. There were others who shared this concern.

'What makes you say so?'

'I've been talking to the Foreign Secretary's driver and he has been talking to the Secretary of State for Trade's driver.'

'And I suppose they have a draft of the text of the statement in their possession.'

'As a matter of fact they have, Me Lord.'

Lord Mafeking stared ahead as the car turned into the Strand. In a curious way he was not surprised by Sergeant Banger or what he had just said.

'The revised draft of the statement is in the envelope on the parcel shelf, if you'd care to look at it, Me Lord.'

Lord Mafeking opened the brown envelope and began to read.

'The offending parts were in paragraphs two and five, Me Lord. The first draft para two clearly gave the impression that force reduction decisions taken by our Ministry had contributed significantly to a feeling in the minds of the Marranesian leadership that we would not react physically to an invasion. All such references have been taken out in the second draft and by and large it's about all right. I hope you agree, Me Lord.'

'Er ... yes, of course, quite right.' Lord Mafeking was still trying to understand paragraph one, but Sergeant Banger certainly appeared to be on the right track.

'By the same token, I thought it made more sense to have a positive reference alongside mention of HMS *Reluctance*, Me

Lord. Talk about where she is going now, rather than refer back to old decisions.'

'Did the Foreign Secretary's driver agree these changes?'

'After a bit of persuasion, Me Lord. After all, he wants me to put his new central heating in for him next weekend.'

'So that's what it turned on, then?'

'I should think so, Me Lord. After all, us drivers have to keep our feet on the ground and be practical men of the world. We leave the theoretical stuff to you, Me Lord.'

Sergeant Banger smiled ever so quietly to himself while Lord Mafeking stared unblinkingly at the document. He wasn't reading it. He didn't need to read it. There was no real need for him to read anything ever again because good old Sergeant Banger would see to it. Sergeant Banger would converse with the other drivers throughout the ranks of MOD and the government car service. Be they Granada drivers or Cortina drivers or Princess drivers, none of them would be beyond the reach of Sergeant Banger and his mates and all of them would be united in the plotting and planning and conniving that went into manoeuvring their Ministers while giving them the illusion that they were in charge.

Lord Mafeking thought suddenly of Brian, whom he would presently be seeing, and Jolyon.

'Did the Private Office type the second draft?' asked Lord Mafeking, trying to sound casual but beginning to wonder if the typing might not have been done by Sergeant Banger's sister Karen in Maida Vale.

'Oh yes, Me Lord,' and then Sergeant Banger went on as if aware of the doubt in his Lordship's mind. 'I find the Private Office are very obliging where I'm concerned. Brian and his wife breed rare budgies and I seem to have cornered the market in the feed they find essential. So no co-operation, no feed, no budgies. And as for Jolyon, I have enough on him to last a lifetime. He's a transvestite. Danny La Rue of MOD. His drawers are packed with drawers.'

The car was about to turn into Chancellor's Gate at the House of Lords. Lord Mafeking felt that he should have been thinking deep philosophical thoughts about the drivers' connection, the mysterious network that really ran the country. If British drivers knew Marrancsian drivers perhaps the invasion wouldn't have happened. If Brezhnev's driver was on first name terms with Reagan's driver maybe the world would be a safer place, and then again it might not be. Instead of thinking such thoughts, Lord Mafeking adjusted his hearing aid, smiled awkwardly at Sergeant Banger and marched off into the House of Lords.

3

The Delegation Divides

♦

GENERAL HERNANDO, Commander of the invading Marranesian Army, could not have been nicer. He was particularly courteous and solicitous to Rosie Long. She and the other MPs were escorted to the Air Traffic Control office, where seats were provided and they were given a chance to freshen up.

Rosie Long began to feel somewhat restored. A small tot of brandy which she carried in her handbag for 'accident situations' had come in very handy. She looked at the General, who was quite tall for a Marranesian and had sleek dark hair and a long handsome face. Rosie had introduced the members of the delegation to the General, who had saluted each member in turn.

'I very much regret that you have been inconvenienced in this way,' the General began as they sat round in a circle in the small office. 'If it had not been for the weather, you would have been safely on your way. I am now responsible for your safe return to your country. Now that the annexation and reunification of these islands with Marranesia is complete, the arrangements for civilian rule will be put in hand. Your Royal Marines, whom we have captured after very good resistance, will be flown to a third country for onward flights to Britain and I would think that this will also happen to all of you. I know that you will have very important business in the Mother of Parliaments and I will not detain you longer than necessary to make the arrangements.'

As this produced no response from the group, the General continued, 'Subject to your approval, I would propose that we go to Government House, where there is accommodation and you can reoccupy the rooms you used last night. I will come to Government House this evening and we can discuss the arrangements in more detail. The plan would be for the former

Governor to leave on the same plane as yourselves. Have you any questions?'

Rosie felt it incumbent on her to ask the question on all their minds. 'How long will it be before we fly out?'

'About two or three days at the most. If there are no further questions, I suggest we move now to Government House.'

Three jeep type vehicles were drawn up outside and the General and two of his staff rode with the delegation back into Port Roger. The flag of Marranesia flew briskly over Government House and a sentry in an olive green uniform saluted smartly as they filed inside.

In the drawing room the Governor and his wife stood up as the delegation entered.

'My dear Mrs Long,' said the Governor, seizing her hand, unaware of Rosie's recent repeat performance. 'Are you all right?' He sought reassurance from each delegation member. Wentworth Stringer was fool enough to ask how he was. The Governor simply nodded silently in reply, conscious that General Hernando was in the room.

'I will come back to see you after dinner. I am sure you will all have plenty to talk about.' The General smiled slightly, saluted and left. Rosie thought he was rather attractive. There was complete silence in the room and the three Army vehicles could be heard driving away.

Once again the delegation from the Mother of Parliaments was seated in a circle on either side of the former Governor. Each of them looked at the former Governor and he looked at them. In the movies this was the moment for John Mills or Trevor Howard or David Niven to say something dramatic, but no-one in the drawing room at Government House seemed to want to audition for the part. Kelp brought in some coffee on a tray and a few moments were taken with distributing the cups round the room. When this was complete, Kelp remained on the hover in a corner of the room. The former Governor broke the silence.

'I really am most terribly sorry about all this,' he wailed. 'When the firing started, my one and only consolation was that you had got away in the nick of time. The Marranesians must have known about your visit and timed their invasion accordingly.'

'They seemed to have known about rather a lot,' observed

Rollo Herbert-Fitzherbert dryly. Mr Cunningham, the former Governor, did not comment or respond to the implied criticism, but sighed the sigh of a man who had been forced to surrender on film and photograph and have his national flag taken down and the flag of a hated invader raised in its place.

'There must be a hell of a row going on in the House,' said Wentworth Stringer.

Rosie Long laughed. 'Roars upon roars of righteous indignation. Bench after bench of furious red faces. Someone will already have been sacked as the price of this humiliation. Tory discomfiture is worth going a long way to see and this will be mega-discomfiture.' She rubbed her hands with glee.

'There is a well-established convention that when abroad we put our party differences on one side in the interests of national solidarity,' snapped Wentworth Stringer harshly.

'I don't need any lectures from you, Wentworth, on what is expected of us when taking a parliamentary delegation abroad,' responded Rosie, on her high horse. 'Besides, there is a perfectly good case for saying that the national interest lies in allowing the Faraway Islands to make their future with their Marranesian neighbours and not cling on to a relationship with a distant colonial power on the other side of the world.'

Wentworth Stringer looked as though he might explode. His face was crimson with fury and his prominent eyebrows seemed to be bristling and crackling as though with static electricity.

'What!' he shrieked. Former Governor Cunningham attempted to make a truce but was brushed aside.

'You sit here, Rosie Long, as the leader of a delegation from the British Parliament and are prepared to acquiesce — because that is all I can make of your outrageous remarks — acquiesce in and condone the invasion by a member of the United Nations on the territory of another UN member. This is scandalous!'

'No, I do not support the use of force and I am relieved that the Governor has told us that there were no British casualties. I regret the deaths of the Marranesians who have apparently been killed during the invasion,' Rosie hit back, defiant as ever. 'What I am saying is there are many people in Britain who think we should have got out of this sort of colonial entanglement years ago when we had some claim to be a great power. What on earth is the point of our being responsible for fifteen hundred people whose only claim on this is that their DNA structure proves that they are direct descendants from the original all-British settlers.'

'This is very good debating stuff, Rosie,' weighed in Rollo Herbert-Fitzherbert, 'but the absolutely fundamental point remains that no matter what the merits of the arguments concerning the future of the Faraway Islands, the situation cannot be sorted out by force. That cannot be tolerated. Don't you agree, George?'

'I most certainly do,' said Lord Hogshead. 'If territorial disputes in places a long way off are going to be allowed to be settled by force, then world order as we know it is in jeopardy.' Rosie shot a glance at Albert Blackhead. 'What do you think, Albert?'

Albert Blackhead shuffled uneasily in his chair. He did not like being asked for an opinion on anything, particularly when he was not going to be able to follow his leader's line of thinking. 'I agree with the others. We cannot have the Marranesians take these islands because that tells any dictator he can go ahead and do the same.'

Rosie snorted. 'Albert Blackhead, you're a blockhead. I never thought I'd hear you parroting this Tory Liberal claptrap about the sanctity of the United Nations. What about the Palestinians and UN Resolution 242, may I ask? Yes, you all go silent on that one, I notice. Sauce for the goose is sauce for the gander.'

'Anyway,' Rosie continued defiantly, 'this is all academic because the Marranesians are here to stay and we had better get used to it. Like it or not, the facts have changed and so has the *de facto* ownership. No way is the Tory Government going to do anything about it.'

'That, my dear,' Wentworth Stringer did not in any way mean the endearment. His tone was icy and gave Rosie a twinge of alarm, 'is exactly where you are wrong. If you imagine for one moment that our Prime Minister will put up with this, then you are profoundly mistaken.'

'Hear, hear,' chimed in Rollo Herbert-Fitzherbert.

'I don't think I'm hearing this,' said Rosie. Again former Governor Cunningham took in breath to indicate he would like to contribute and again he was waved into silence by Rosie.

'You are telling me that the Tory Government will send an armada eight thousand miles to recapture these Islands by force? You can't be serious?!'

'I've never been more serious in my life,' replied Wentworth Stringer. 'And I think it's high time you came to your senses, accepted the realities of the situation and considered the seriousness of your personal position.'

'What on earth do you mean, Wentworth?'

'I mean, Rosie, that you are the leader of a British parliamentary delegation which has become caught up in a war situation, or at the very least a conflict situation. If you continue to express the views you have, which amount to a condoning of the annexation of these islands by force, you are actually giving aid and comfort to an enemy and I know what that means, even if you don't.'

'Don't you dare threaten me, Wentworth Stringer. If that is to be your attitude, you might like to know that while I do not support the use of force by Marranesia or Britain or anyone else — and I say that because Britain can't do anything these days without help from the United States — I do support the aims and objectives of the Marranesian Marxist Revolution. That can't surprise you. I am a Marxist. I have always been a Marxist and I always will be a Marxist. I support the Marranesian people. They wish to extend their freedom to this backward colonial outpost. Well, that's fine with me.' Rosie had leapt to her feet, her face shining, exultant at her declaration of faith. All the years of fudging, composite trade union compromise motions, appeasing the Right in the Labour Party, all this had fallen away in a glorious chest-clearing reaffirmation of socialism red in tooth and claw, and she felt wonderful.

All politicians start off with a set of beliefs and ideals. It's as they progress through the labyrinths of the possible and the achievable that their original cutting edge is blunted. Rarely do any of them get the chance to make a restatement of basic beliefs. This was what was so special for Rosie Long. She had never seen herself as a modern-day Passionara, or even a Barbara Castle, but she knew her Geordie people and she loved them and they her.

Rosie now felt able to conclude her affirmation of faith. 'I have always felt contempt for those people who won't stand up and fight for their beliefs whatever those beliefs are and regardless of whether I share them or not. General Hernando has said that he is making arrangements to fly us out in two or three days. When he returns this evening at around nine o'clock I intend to tell him that I have formally relinquished the leadership of the parliamentary delegation and handed over to Wentworth Stringer. I do not intend to return to the UK at this time. I wish to remain here for the time being to help in any way I can the fulfilment of the Marranesian Revolution. I am now going to my room and I look forward to seeing you all later when the General arrives.'

That said, Rosie Long gathered her handbag and thin briefcase and swept out of the room, followed by the former Governor, who wanted to see that she would be all right in her room.

There was silence for a moment, but only a moment, and then Wentworth Stringer leapt to his feet.

'I think we all know now where we stand. The situation appears to be as follows. The Marranesians will keep us here in this house in comfortable and genteel house arrest for two or three days until we are flown out with the former Governor and the Royal Marines to a third country and thence on to the UK. Rosie Long has declared herself to be a Quisling, ready and willing to betray the interests of her country. I am sure her constituents will be most interested to hear about her involvement in due course.'

'Those of us in this room have two options. One is to return on the plane as planned by the Marranesians, or the other is to do what I propose, which is to slip away and help the islanders co-ordinate their resistance until such time as the Task Force gets here. It will take a Task Force at least three weeks to get here from the time they can get under way, which means virtually a month for the islanders to get organised, re-establish the intelligence network and carry out active operations against the enemy. One of our first tasks will be to get radio contact going with the outside world and in particular London. I have had a word with Kelp before this meeting began and he is ready to come with us and take us to the leaders of the island community.'

At that moment former Governor Cunningham re-entered the room and resumed his seat. Wentworth Stringer gave him a careful and sustained stare.

'Mr Cunningham, I have summarised the situation while you were not in the room. Mrs Long has made her position clear and will have to live with the consequences. The choices for the rest of us are to go on the Marranesian plane to be repatriated or to stay here and join the resistance.'

'Oh! Dear me!' exclaimed Cunningham. 'Stay here and join the resistance,' he repeated.

'Which is what I intend to do,' said Wentworth Stringer, in case there should be any doubt.

'Quite so, quite so,' said Cunningham. 'I am sure Kelp will have some good ideas - won't you, Kelp?' Kelp gave a rather delphic smile from his vantage point in one corner of the room. 'Of course you will appreciate that I can't possibly join your enterprise. As the former Commander-in-Chief of Forces on these islands, I must leave with the forces who have surrendered. I cannot become a sort of Robin Hood. The Foreign Office would not approve of that at all.'

Wentworth Stringer had in mind the crack about wondering which side the Foreign Office was on, but decided against any snide remarks. In any case, he was not enamoured at the prospect of being joined in his commando-style operation by former Governor Cunningham. To him Cunningham would be a major encumbrance.

'I am sure we all understand your position, Mr Cunningham. The best thing you can do is to get back and tell the story of this naked and unprovoked aggression and tell it as widely as you can, not just in our own country but overseas, especially in the United States. That is a vital role in mobilising world public opinion in our support. I am sure we all wish you well. I need to know who else will join me and stay here.'

Rollo Herbert-Fitzherbert was the first. 'You can count me in, Wentworth,' he said.

'Good. What about you, George?' Wentworth Stringer looked at Lord Hogshead.

'Wentworth, I'd like to very much but I don't think I should. As you already know, my feet are not in good shape and quite frankly, I would be a bloody liability the first time you had to do anything remotely physical. I really am sad, but I wish you all the luck in the world and it will be helpful to have someone in our

House who can speak from direct personal experience. The first time Lord Mafeking tries to put one over on me, I'll bop him one.' They all laughed. Wentworth Stringer was not upset. George Hogshead was a good chap, but he was very out of condition and his self-assessment was perfectly realistic.

'What about you, Albert?' Wentworth Stringer asked Albert Blackhead, who sat in his armchair running a finger along the rim of his brown trilby hat which he had on his lap.

'You've spoken about three options. Well, I'm certainly not following Rosie Long's lead. I think she's very, very wrong and very foolish ...' — 'Hear, hear,' cut in Rollo Herbert-Fitzherbert — 'and I think she'll lose the Labour movement a lot of support.' Albert usually spoke of the Labour movement rather than the Labour Party. 'The patriotism of the Labour movement has not been called in question in two World Wars and nor will it be now. Our members have served in the front lines and the factories, so we can be counted on. My choice is whether to be repatriated or to stay with you, Wentworth. On balance I would prefer to stay, even though I am not fantastically fit, nor am I sure what I can do, but I'm with you.' The warm Yorkshire voice sounded strong and comforting. Wentworth Stringer was very pleased and he showed it.

'That is terrific, Albert. Thank you so much. I agree with what you said about the Labour movement and patriotism. No-one in my party has any reason to doubt that concepts of loyalty to the Queen and country are deeply held in the Labour movement. I am particularly glad that if three of us are to join the resistance we are not all from one political party. That will help to reinforce the all-party nature of our actions. Now that I know everyone's intentions, my inclination is that we should act very quickly. Those joining the resistance should have left before the General comes here this evening. Would you agree, Mr Cunningham?'

'Yes I would. If you stay, the General will quickly guess what is on your mind once a discussion starts concerning Mrs Long's plans. I am not, incidentally, absolutely sure that the General will allow Mrs Long to remain. She could be a great inconvenience at best, or an embarrassment at worst. He will probably have to signal his capital for approval. As far as you are concerned, Kelp will take you by way of the secret passage which connects the basement with a guest house outside the compound. That should enable you to get clear. I think the secret passage was built in the time of one of my predecessors called Bonker Bowman, who had a lady at the guest house. Usually he went there but occasionally she came here, which was his undoing in the end. I'll tell you about it when we are together in happier times, as I am sure we will be. More immediately, Kelp should help you with proper clothing and especially footwear. You know that we are coming into our winter which is as grim as the summer, only worse. The winds are stronger and the rain heavier. Kelp must concentrate on waterproof and windproof kit because I appreciate that a parliamentary delegation does not equip itself to live off the land for a month.'

Cunningham was rising in Wentworth Stringer's estimation. He was being clear-thinking and decisive, not at all the pathetic crushed figure of even a few hours ago.

'I'm grateful to you, Mr Cunningham, for your advice. I think that all of us should now go to our rooms with Kelp and get together whatever kit we can. I think it would look better, George, if you too came with us to our rooms just in case the General comes early and gets suspicious. If no-one is here with Mr Cunningham he is less likely to find that odd. Also, George, I will have a letter for you to give to the Prime Minister on your return. Therefore, Mr Cunningham, we will take our leave and wish you and your wife a safe return to England and my colleagues and I look forward to entertaining you at the House and also to being received by you here when the Union flag flies above Government House, as it surely will.'

'Sir Wentworth, I admire what you are doing enormously and I wish you Godspeed from the bottom of my heart. How I wish I could be with you. I have a bottle of whisky here in addition to the one which Kelp is taking for you. I think we should drink a toast.' Kelp quickly charged the glasses. 'God save the Queen.' 'The Queen,' and then, 'To the recapture of the Faraway Islands.' 'To the recapture.'

The glasses were emptied and one by one they shook hands with former Governor Cunningham and followed Kelp into the hall and upstairs to their rooms. Cunningham went in search of his wife, who had been very shocked by the whole invasion and was lying down in their room.

Dinner had been set for eight o'clock on the assumption that the General would appear some time after nine. Cunningham was ready in the drawing room to entertain anyone who might appear and want a drink before dinner. He was presently joined by Mrs Cunningham, who had made a valiant effort to facelift her spirits into a *Rule Britannia* mode, and, shortly afterwards, Rosie Long entered, having changed from her day suit into a floral print dress.

'I'll have a sweet sherry, please. Am I the first?'

Kelp filled her glass and switched on the hot plate on the sideboard. The main course would be served from the hot plate by the cook as Kelp had arranged to have the evening off and the cook was doubling up. Little did the cook know just how long the doubling up would last. George Hogshead appeared and received his pre-prandial medication. As there was still no sign of the others, Kelp went into the hall and sounded the gong.

'I think we should go ahead. Dinner's ready and I'm sure the others won't be long,' Cunningham said with fake confidence. He seated Rosie Long on his right, his wife on his left and George Hogshead opposite. Kelp filled the wine glasses and went into the hall. The first course, a pâté, was already on the plates in front of the diners so there was no need to do anything else in the dining room. Kelp closed the dining room door behind him and took the few steps across the hall to the boot room packed with coats, hats and assorted walking sticks. From among the coats stepped Sir Wentworth Stringer, Rollo Herbert-Fitzherbert and Albert Blackhead, and they quickly followed Kelp to the end of the hall, turned left sharply through a door and down a flight of steps into the basement. Kelp moved the empty wardrobe which stood in front of a stable door. He reached inside, unbolted the door and switched on his torch.

Back in the dining room conversation was flagging somewhat. 'Where on earth can the others be, I wonder?' asked Rosie Long as the cook prepared to clear the pâté plates and to serve the main course from the hot plate. 'I know we had a bit of a dust-up earlier but it isn't like Wentworth Stringer to harbour a grudge, or the others either. If I had a ten pound note for every time I've called Albert Blackhead a blockhead I'd be a very rich lady indeed by now. What do you think, George, is this some sort of loyalist boycott of dinner?'

Lord Hogshead waved his hands dismissively. 'I don't think anyone took offence at what was said earlier. After all, if a British parliamentary delegation can't have a frank and free exchange of views, then things are coming to a pretty pass.'

'Fair enough, but where are they then?' persisted Rosie. 'For all I know they may have had something taken up to their rooms.'

'Kelp would know, but he's got the evening off,' responded Lord Hogshead, much to the admiration of Governor Cunningham.

'Oh well. I prefer to be sociable. A sociable socialist.' Mrs Cunningham laughed as though the very idea was derisory.

'As long as they're here for the General,' said Rosie as they concluded the main course, enjoyed the cheese and then adjourned back to the drawing room for coffee.

They were not there when the General arrived at nearly half past nine and was shown into the drawing room by the cook. Once again the General was the essence of courtesy and good manners, seeking to put everyone at their ease, but Rosie was clearly at a loss to explain the poor attendance.

'Before the others join us, General, I want to make a short statement and I'm sorry if that sounds a touch pompous, but I can't think of another word to describe what I want to say.' The General smiled and indicated by his friendly hand movements that there was no problem and she should proceed. 'General Hernando. I do not want to be evacuated with the Governor and the others. I want to stay and do what I can to help you and the Marranesian Government at this very difficult time. You will have to deal with an English-speaking population of British stock who are in a state of shock and will need sympathetic guidance and understanding. I can play that role either up-front on the radio or in the background advising you. I know that many people in my own country will misunderstand my motives, but I can tell you that lots of people are much more sympathetic to the Marranesian claim on these islands than you might imagine. I strongly believe that the matter can be resolved without further bloodshed and that is what I want.'

The General was seated in an armchair directly across from Rosie Long. In her floral dress she looked very attractive, particularly the way her face seemed to shine with her commitment to what she was saying. The General was very surprised at what he heard. None of the Secret Intelligence briefings had prepared him for this kind of response. He almost suspected a trap, except that Rosie was obviously utterly sincere in what she believed and what she said.

'Thank you for what you have said,' the General began in reply. Rosie noticed that he liked to rub the back of his left hand with his right fingers if he seemed in any way surprised and unsure of himself. 'I must confess that I was not expecting anyone to say what you have said. You have shown such wisdom and insight that I can only hope your lead will be followed from London. I am also deeply grateful for your offer of help, which I personally would welcome. You will understand, of course, that as a soldier my orders are to protect you and to ensure your safe return to your country. I will send a message to my government later tonight asking for their instructions, which I should have tomorrow. If you stay here you will not be able to report the conclusion of your delegation to Parliament?' The General's tone was quiet and quizzical.

'That's true,' answered Rosie. 'And there is a case for my going back and fighting my corner as someone who has been there, but I have a pretty good idea what the atmosphere will be like in London right now. There will be no chance of a reasoned argument. It will be jingoism all the way. I think I can serve the cause of peace best by being here. I have already handed over leadership of the delegation to Sir Wentworth Stringer.'

'Might I ask where is Sir Wentworth and his two colleagues?' The General was mildly curious.

Lord Hogshead spoke. 'I think this might clarify matters,' he said, taking a letter from his inside jacket pocket and handing it to Rosie Long. Rosie opened the letter and began to read. It was from Wentworth Stringer.

> *Dear Rosie,*
> *You know how much I regret your decision not to return to the UK and, instead, to stay and ally yourself to the Marranesian*

cause. Much though I respect your beliefs and principles, I believe that you are seriously in error in this case.

No matter how strong a case the Marranesians believe they have in claiming the Faraway Islands, they have no justification whatsoever for using military force in pursuit of their claim. You know what I am saying is correct and no amount of weasel wording can change that.

I wonder also, equally seriously, whether you have given any thought to the nature and reputation of the regime whose cause you are to support so publicly. You know of the mothers whose teenage children have disappeared, believed murdered by the regime, and you know of the Amnesty International report condemning the use of torture on political prisoners.

My two colleagues, Arthur and Rollo, and I share your view in one regard only. We also will not be on the evacuation flight. By the time you read this we will have linked up with elements of the resistance on the Islands and we shall work with that resistance until the Islands are freed.

Mark my words. The government of Marranesia has made a serious error of judgment. Their presence on the Faraway Islands will end. Their cause is doomed. Our concern is for you, our colleague. There is still time for you to change your mind.

The Task Force inevitably will contain men and women who are sons and daughters or brothers and uncles of your constituents. What are your constituents going to say when they realise that you have actively worked for the enemy?

If you continue with your course of action your name will go down in history as worse than Mata Hari — a sort of female Lord Haw Haw. Treachery to your country, to which you owe everything, will make your name stink as long as the English language is spoken. We pray for you,

Yours ever,
Wentworth

Rosie had flushed and her mouth tightened as she read the letter. Without comment she handed the letter to the General, who also read it in silence before he handed it to Cunningham and got to his feet.

'So the British desire to support lost causes continues. In one way I should be reassured, even happy, that this beguiling national trait still exists in the last two decades of the twentieth century. But my real concern, Mrs Long, is for your three colleagues. The Islands are windswept and inhospitable. They will only be able to move at night to avoid detection. They are not in the peak of physical condition. They will fall into ditches and get stuck in bogs. I want my men to find them quickly and bring them back to the safety and warmth of Government House. Minefields will be laid which will make it very dangerous to move about in unapproved areas. Sir Wentworth's assessment is fundamentally wrong. Each day more of our troops plus heavy equipment are flown in. Our position gets stronger every day. No Task Force can dislodge us and because this fact is well appreciated in London, no Task Force will come.'

Three miles away on the outskirts of Port Roger Arthur Blackhead fell into a ditch up to his waist and had to be pulled out by the others. A long dark waterlogged road lay ahead.

4

No-one was Really to Blame

♦

STATEMENTS WERE MADE IN BOTH HOUSES the following morning at eleven. In the Commons the Foreign Secretary attempted to describe what was happening, but he was hampered by the fact that the communication links with the Faraway Islands were variable and it could not be definitely confirmed that the invasion had happened.

Later on that same Friday irrefutable confirmation of the invasion was received in London and a wave of indignation began to sweep the lobbies, tea-rooms and the smoking room. Far more Members were still around the House than would be customary on a Friday. Word came that the House would sit at eleven the following day, the first Saturday sitting for many years.

It was unseasonably hot and sunny for April as Arthur Mafeking attacked the daily stubble on his chin and listened to a Tory backbencher demanding that there must be a resignation. The *Today* programme on Radio 4 had put on a 'crisis special' and all shades of opinion were being transmitted over the nation's breakfast cornflakes. There was already speculation as to where the blame most properly should be placed. The prime contenders for this accolade were the Foreign Office and the Ministry of Defence, although of the two the Foreign Office would be most distrusted, particularly by the Tory Right.

Arthur, second Viscount Mafeking, reflected that he would be very lucky to come through this crisis with his political life intact. He knew that many Tories resented Peers in government, although he was never certain precisely of the reasons. Perhaps it had something to do with the fact that every Peer in government represented an advancement opportunity lost to a Member of the House of Commons. In his own case he had not gone out of his way to win over his Commons colleagues. To him they tended to look alike — he had difficulty in hearing what they said or in remembering their names.

There had never been any political tradition in his family, his father having been ennobled for doing a good job in keeping the ration convoys moving in the Boer War. When his father had said that the peerage had 'come up with the rations' there was more than a grain of truth in it.

Arthur had a good war in the Blues and was decorated for 'conspicuous gallantry', although this only after a prolonged enquiry decided narrowly in his favour. At one time it was in the balance whether he was sacked, promoted, decorated or court martialled. Certainly his appalling map-reading and non-existent sense of direction led him to take his tank for dinner with the German Panzer Commander on more than one occasion and had the effect of demoralising the neighbouring American armoured formations.

After the war Arthur went into timber, which many people thought highly appropriate. The company managed to survive having had him on its Board of Directors and this enabled him to lecture captains of the defence electronic industries on the right ways of running their businesses.

His marriage to Lady Mafeking was probably a mistake, although she had never let him down in public. He kept her fed and watered and periodically serviced and she seemed content, as far as he could tell. Her voice had grown more shrill as she passed through the change of life sound barrier and it now occupied an upper part of the decibel range that it was almost impossible for Arthur Lord Mafeking to detect, let alone comprehend. He would become aware of a sound that he remembered as being rather like a circular saw when he could hear circular saws and then he would notice that Lady Mafeking's lips were moving. He had developed a technique over the years which involved nodding and grunting and then patting her firmly on the head with a piece of buttered toast. If it happened to be near the time in the quarter when her servicing was due, he might well playfully drop a piece of buttered toast down the inside of her blouse. This aroused Lady Mafeking to unparalleled heights of desire and by the time he returned from the Lords that evening, he could well find her swinging gently from the drawing room chandelier clad only in her coronation tiara. A quick burst with the fire extinguisher usually restored the situation.

On the morning of the great debate he noticed that Lady Mafeking's lips were moving, but he was in a hurry and had no time to butter toast for eating, let alone for other purposes. As he picked up his red ministerial box in the hall, Lady Mafeking screeched from her perch in the kitchen and then he was gone, off to face an increasingly hostile world.

At the Parliament building long queues waited to gain admittance at St Stephen's entrance. In all probability their wait would be in vain because tickets would be obtained by Members and officers of the House and given out to their families and friends.

Lord Mafeking left his red box in his office at the Lords and started to make his way from the plush port-wine colours of his House across the great Central Lobby to the Commons, with its workaday green livery. In the Members' Lobby there was a tremendous hubbub as Members gossiped with one another. On either side of the Lobby the message boards were a blaze of lights, indicating the presence of phone messages and written messages for Members. The country was starting to raise its voice about the invasion of the Faraway Islands in no uncertain terms. All around the Lobby the statues of Churchill, Lloyd George and Attlee gazed down on the making of history as the House once more gathered to consider issues of war and peace.

Peers have the front two rows of the public gallery reserved for them. Lord Mafeking sat down on the front row next to Lord Mollusc and surveyed the cauldron below.

He had long been surprised as to the degree to which members of the various parties in the Commons conformed to the stereotypical pictures of them. It was almost as though it was an article of faith to do so, or alternatively some secret standing order ordained it.

So many of the Tories really did have pin-striped suits and nice crinkly hair, often fashionably white. So many Labour Members obviously slept in their suits, pausing in the morning only to change their socks, one red and one orange. Labour women (Lord Mafeking could not possibly call them ladies) seemed to have all put their clothes on in the same wind tunnel. Liberals came in all shapes and sizes and the SDP, still fighting to get seats below the gangway among the Tribune Group, were as yet displaying no discernible physical type.

Lord Mafeking looked down on the government front bench and the row of famous names with features so beloved of the cartoonists. Not an inch of space could be found for any latecomers. The overflow galleries above each side of the House were full. The Press Gallery and the Public Gallery were packed. The Government Chief Whip sat on the seat next to the gangway on the front bench, supporting his head with his hand. The Deputy Chief Whip squatted in the aisle alongside his Chief and another senior Whip sat behind the Chief.

The Speaker called for order and then called the Foreign Secretary to speak. Lord Mafeking noticed that the Prime Minister was looking particularly stony-faced at the Foreign Secretary's side, and what is more she had placed her dark blue handbag on the table close to the despatch box. The dark blue handbag was rumoured to contain some billets of cement and its presence near the despatch box was widely seen as an unfavourable sign.

The Foreign Secretary glanced quickly at the Speaker, almost as though he half expected that worthy to have vacated his chair already. He coughed and cleared his throat. He was a small man who tended to tuck his head into his chest when speaking, thus giving an impression that he had no neck and that his eyes were somewhere near the top of his head.

'Mr Speaker. This must be one of the gravest days in the history of this House. The grave news from the south Pacific serves only to heighten and to underscore the gravity of the situation. Before I say anything else, I must express the profound concern of all Right Honourable and Honourable Members of this House for the safety and welfare of our colleagues who are members of a delegation of this House to the Faraway Islands. We know that their aircraft returned to Port Roger with engine trouble, only to find that the Islands had been invaded. I have to tell the House, therefore, that one of our delegations is missing.

'The information we have is still sketchy because all contact with Port Roger ceased at 08.15 local time yesterday. In one of the last messages received, the Governor of the Faraway Islands, Mr Cunningham, said that an invasion by Marranesian forces was taking place and was being resisted.

'In the Foreign Office we occasionally take pride in not knowing what is going on, because in that way it is impossible for us to be subverted or led astray or fed false information, because if we are not in the business of acquiring information in the first place it matters little whether it is true or false information. To know what is going on can betray a dangerous sense of commitment and interest and give rise to wholly unwarranted assumptions and aspirations concerning the intentions of Her Majesty's Government. There are so many virtues in not knowing — the American slang phrase "in the know" has negative overtones and one could go so far as to describe the Foreign Office position as "ignorance is bliss".'

By now the House was much quieter because they sensed that they were listening to a progressively light-headed speech from the scaffold. The collective rage had eased and nostrils were now twitching in all parts of the House as a ritual resignation sacrifice loomed in sight. The Prime Minister had moved and moved again her handbag in a vain attempt to keep the Foreign Secretary in touch with the straight and narrow of the government position. To the Foreign Secretary, however, it seemed that the Elysian gates of freedom were opening up in front of his eyes as the bondage of office loosened. He gripped the edges of the despatch box and stared unseeing at the pages of his Foreign Office brief laid out in a folder on top.

'It has been said that modern communication has made the world a global village. There are, however, parts of the village where communication is less good than others.

'We are in contact with the Secretary General of the United Nations with a view to seeking an urgent early meeting of the Security Council. We are seeking an early meeting of the Foreign Ministers of our fellow European Community partners with the intention of enlisting their firm support for any action we may decide to take.'

'*May* decide?' shouted an incredulous Tory backbencher, and the word *may* was taken up as a growling, snarling chorus, rippling and surging to and fro along the packed benches. The

Foreign Secretary glanced anxiously half behind him to left and right, aware that he had set off a landmine in the midst of the field of explosive sentiment in which he now stood. Any word he uttered was derided, any silence was akin to appeasement and defeatism.

The Chairman of the Tory Back Bench Defence Committee rose in his seat, gold watch chain at his waistcoat and monocle in his left eye. He asked the Foreign Secretary to give way, which the Foreign Secretary did, sinking like a doomed puppet among the iceberg friendship of his front bench colleagues.

'Is my Right Honourable Friend aware that this House,' bellowed Sir Arthur Shrapnel, 'is less interested in the niceties of Foreign Office protocol concerning confirmation of statements made, when it is perfectly obvious to all the world that the British Faraway Islands have been invaded by an aggressor, but more interested — indeed, may I say, vitally interested — in knowing what the government *will* decide to do about it?'

The emphasis on the word *will*, in contrast to the Foreign Secretary's *may*, could have appeared almost pedantic on any other occasion than this, but the House of Commons in this mood brooks no opposition and is incapable of reasoned argument. As a piece of theatre it was superb, for drama unrivalled — how the broadcasting companies longed for television cameras to augment their live sound broadcasts — and as the destruction of the political career of an honourable man, it was appalling. There was not a seat to be had anywhere in the House.

At the despatch box, the Foreign Secretary had taken on the appearance of a dismasted schooner attempting to round Cape Horn, shipping water by the sentence.

'I can assure my Honourable Friend and the House that a statement on the government's intentions will be made very soon.' Cries of 'When?'

'That is not a matter for me to decide. I am sure that my Right Honourable Friend the Prime Minister may — er.. will — probably, wish to make an early statement.' Here he glanced uneasily at the Presence to his left. 'As far as the dispositions of our armed forces are concerned, that is a matter for my Noble Friend, the Secretary of State for Defence.' Here, there was some underground muttering, such as always greeted the mention of

Lord Mafeking's official title. 'But I can tell the House,' went on the Foreign Secretary in one last dying flurry, 'that one of our nuclear submarines is already en route for the Faraways. The Fleet has been ordered to make ready.'

This almost Napoleonic-sounding announcement raised a genuine cheer of approval and relief, expressed in the characteristic 'yere, yere, yere' that Members of Parliament use on such occasions. The Foreign Secretary had more padding and Foreign Office waffle still to deliver in his folder but, sensing that this cheer was as good an out-line as he was likely to get, he sat down at once on the Prime Minister's lap. For what seemed an age he perched there like a ventriloquist's dummy.

Lord Mafeking decided that he had had as much as he could take and as the Shadow Foreign Secretary rambled through his battery of questions, he slipped along the front row of the gallery, made his way down the stairs to the Members' Lobby and headed for his room in the House of Lords.

Once the Foreign Secretary had phoned, Lord Mafeking left his own office and walked along the House of Lords corridor, passed the dining room, and presently exchanged the magenta plushness of their Lordships' House for the workaday drabness of House of Commons green.

'Come in, Arthur. Have a drink. We'll both need one.' The Foreign Secretary was as affable as ever. He was a decent chap, who had always been kind to Lord Mafeking. They had known each other slightly at Eton and he'd had a good war. The Foreign Secretary had with him the Minister of State for the Armed Forces, who answered on defence matters in the Commons with his boss being in the Lords. This was Thomas Scintilla — known as Doubting Tom — a tall, lean figure with a permanently anxious air about him. He was reputed to drive his officials nearly insane with repeated requests for absurd levels of detail.

'Were you in the House for my statement?'

'Yes.'

'Well, it was a pretty good dress rehearsal for the 22. As you saw, the party's mood could not be uglier. Their blood lust is up and they won't be satisfied until they've got my head on a plate.'

He paused and looked out of the window down at the fountain in New Palace Yard.

'And that is exactly what they're going to get, not that I'm going to give the bastards the satisfaction of being told. My position is between me and the Prime Minister, but I will resign tonight. My departure will help the government. No doubt about it.'

There was silence as the other two men surveyed their drink glasses and then looked at each other. Lord Mafeking spoke first. 'I think it's a damned shame. But I can't fault your logic.'

'When emotions are running this high, something dramatic has to be done to steady the ship and I think that the resignation of the Foreign Secretary could qualify as dramatic. In any case, I think it's justified. Apart from the fact that something needs to be done, I think the Foreign Office have got it wrong on this issue over months, if not years. That is the risk one always runs when dealing with regimes like Marranesia. To them a negotiated settlement is simply a cosmetic for a sell-out and if negotiations prove prolonged, they become impatient. Their reasoning, after all, is that why should we be expected to fight to recover something which we were in the process of handing over — provided we could safeguard the interests of the islanders — and on which we had a defence force consisting of one detachment of Marines?'

'The real problems will come when we start taking casualties. We're going to need a lot of luck,' said the Defence Secretary.

'In this immediate exercise with the 22, your only vulnerable point is the scrapping of HMS *Reluctance*. They will say that gave the Marranesians another signal that we were pulling out and according to that thesis, they're right. If I were you, I'd blame it on the Foreign Office line.' The Foreign Secretary was being characteristically generous but it wasn't that simple, as even Lord Mafeking well knew.

'Even the Ministry of Defence is part of the government — or so I'm told. Therefore if the policy of disengagement has been wrong — and if it has contributed to this mess, then it obviously has been wrong — we all have a collective responsibility. I will have to consider my own position too.'

Tom Scintilla had a puckered brow.

'The logistic problems of assembling a Task Force are very considerable. We will need at least fifty-three *STUFT* vessels,' he said.

'What on earth are *STUFT* vessels, Tom?' asked his boss.

'Ships taken up from trade. We have a team already identifying suitable UK ships in most of the world's ports.'

'Ah well, it's a great reassurance to know that there is such a mastery of detail in the MOD at this testing time,' said the Foreign Secretary with a gentle smile. He looked at his watch. 'I think its time for us to go and meet the lions.'

The three now retraced their steps down the staircase to the back of the chair and then almost at once ascended another staircase, this time up two flights, past the Hansard Official Report Office and the *Times* room and up onto the Committee corridor. This route brought the trio onto the Committee corridor opposite Committee Room 16. The 1922 Committee always met in Committee Room 14, so they were almost there.

5

Heroic Resistance

♦

GENERAL HERNANDO WAS RIGHT when he described the Islands as windswept and inhospitable. An area the size of Wales with a population of less than two thousand meant inevitably that outside Port Roger there were very few isolated settlements. Natural cover was equally scarce. Fortunately for those who were seeking cover, there were some woods which hugged the banks of a shallow, fast-running river. Rollo Herbert-Fitzherbert thought that the river reminded him of the borders of Scotland.

Kelp had a plan. Kelp had one priceless advantage over both British MPs and Marranesian soldiers. He was local. Kelp's father had been involved with the Faraway Islands Survey and the young Kelp had often been able to accompany his father to the remoter parts of the Islands. He therefore knew the Islands very well and, moreover, knew the people he could trust and the people he could not trust.

Kelp discussed his plan with Wentworth Stringer. The first requirement was to get away from Port Roger before the Marranesians made any movements in or out of the town virtually impossible. At the moment it was still the early days after the invasion. Curfews and rigid sentry patrols had not been effectively imposed as yet. The Marranesians were, after all, in total control of a scattered and notoriously apathetic island population. The official attitude of the Marranesian Army was to be civilised and polite to the locals. They were, after all, the army of liberation, even if they spoke a different language to the people whom they had just liberated.

Leaving Port Roger by road was not an option. Any local vehicles attracted close attention and the roads were stiff with Marranesian troops. Leaving the roads and striking out across country in the dark would have appealed to Kelp, who was a fit, frequent fell walker in his mid-thirties, but he was mindful of being accompanied by three out-of-condition middle-aged men carrying holdalls and suitcases. Progress would be very slow and the risk of twisted ankles very great. At daybreak, spotter aircraft and helicopters would find the group as easy to see as cockroaches on a farmhouse floor.

Kelp's plan involved the use of a boat with outboard engine. The boat belonged to one of Kelp's cousins and was tied up in an inlet which ran down to the bay about a mile outside Port Roger.

None of the MPs had come on this overseas mission — or '*jolly*', as the tabloid press loved to describe them — believing that they would have to live rough for three or four weeks. They were therefore not attired to their best advantage. As they gathered in the cloakroom at Government House, Kelp looked them over. He had been able to beg or borrow anoraks for each of the three and Wentworth Stringer had a soft woolly beret which made him look quite the part. Albert Blackhead was firmly attached to his trilby and had it well crammed onto his head because of the prevailing wind. Rollo Herbert-Fitzherbert had set his heart on an item of Marranesian headwear, preferably an officer's hat, and looked forward to the chance to wear one. Kelp had joined them having served the main course of dinner and was not expected to return to the dining room that evening. Wentworth Stringer took charge.

'We must get under way,' he said, looking at his watch. 'George Hogshead will give Rosie Long my letter in about an hour. The General will know then what we are about. Being the cool, in control, character he likes to think himself, he will not issue any immediate instructions about us until he gets back to his HQ. He will order all his units to find us at first light tomorrow. Our aim now is to get as far away from here as fast as possible.

'Kelp will lead us through the secret underground passage to the Old Post Office, which has the great advantage of being outside the walls and therefore beyond the sentries of Government House. Kelp's friends are due to start in five minutes a bit of a disturbance outside the Barracks, and this should keep the Marranesians stimulated and interested while we are getting away. We should avoid being seen and avoid therefore attracting any kind of interest from anybody. Although I am sure very few of the islanders will want to collaborate with the Marranesians, the less they know about our movements at this stage the better. Kelp will lead us by side streets out of Port Roger. We then have to walk as quickly as we can for about a mile until we come to the inlet where the motor boat is berthed. We will have to row to keep the noise down until we are into the Bay and out of sight of the Port installations. We know of no Marranesian Naval units operating as yet in these waters, but we must expect anything. We will then travel in the boat for about three hours round the coast to a safe haven, where we can consolidate and make a firm base. Any questions?'

No-one had any questions. Wentworth Stringer nodded.

'Kelp takes the lead into the passage using his torch. Keep in touch with the man in front. I will turn off the light in here and pull the door closed behind me. Off we go.'

Kelp moved quickly to the passage door and stepped inside, switching on the torch as he did so. Rollo Herbert-Fitzherbert followed him, and then Albert Blackhead. They followed Kelp along the passage, heads slightly bent because of the low roof. They heard Wentworth Stringer close the door in the cloakroom.

Presently they were out in the street beyond Government House. It was cool and, as always, there was a stiff breeze blowing. Kelp signalled and they all fell into line behind him. About half a mile away to their right and not on their line of march, they could hear a spirited disturbance in progress with shouting and chanting. A lorry full of Marranesian troops came round the corner and they froze and remained motionless. The lorry sped past towards the sound of the disturbance and the four resumed their march.

With twelve hundred souls, Port Roger was never a very massive metropolis. Not much over ten minutes of brisk walking saw the group at the edge of the town, with a final row of clapboard-style houses in front of them and inky blackness behind the houses.

At each street junction Kelp had reconnoitred the ground ahead and waved them on when all was clear. As they passed the last houses, Wentworth Stringer said in a low voice, 'Well done, everyone. All right so far. We stick to the road. Kelp and Rollo on one side. Albert and me on the other. If any vehicle comes along, get off the road very fast and get down out of sight. Let's go.'

They recommenced their march, two on each side of the road as ordered. The road roughly followed the line of the coast and ran in a westerly direction from Port Roger. As the group marched, they could hear the waves on the nearby shore, but there was no moonlight to illuminate the sea or the road. They pressed on without speaking, knowing that the march to the inlet should not take more than twenty minutes, not long enough for Albert's feet to start playing up or Rollo's socks to have concertinad inside his ill-fitting borrowed boots. They had a sense of mission and commitment and everything was going well. Then they heard a rumble in the road ahead of them. Kelp sprang onto a hillock by the roadside, straining his eyes to make out the source of the sound.

'Armoured vehicle! Get down!' he shouted.

Each of them took three or four quick steps to the side and flung themselves down onto the spongy moss at the roadside, scrambling to get into the bracken and away from the vehicle's headlight arc.

Albert was unlucky. The mossy bank onto which he had flopped gave way at once and he fell a further three feet into a rain-filled ditch. He lay dutifully motionless, with his face in a clump of ferns and his mouth full of mud, as the tracks of the armoured vehicle came closer. He now realised what he had got himself into. He was lying face down in an ice-cold, muddy bath, and if he attempted to move he would give his position away and probably be shot on the spot.

By now the armoured personnel carrier had turned the bend in the road and was almost literally on top of them. The engine whined and the tracks roared and rumbled and spat out stones and tussocks. The engine changed gear and they wondered if they had been seen and the vehicle was about to stop, but it continued rumbling on its way and presently vanished in the direction of Port Roger.

Albert felt Wentworth Stringer's hands pulling at his shoulders. Kelp too was at his side, helping the sodden form into the upright position.

'Are you all right?' asked Wentworth Stringer. Albert grunted and nodded and the march resumed.

A further ten minutes' march saw the road veer off inland. Kelp waved the group behind him as they turned off the road and descended a path to what looked like a fast-running river. In fact, some trees which had fallen during a storm had formed a natural pontoon beyond which the river flowed quickly. Inside the fallen tree pontoon was a small boat. Kelp expertly got aboard and, using the oars with skill, brought the boat close to the bank.

Wentworth Stringer and then Rollo clambered into the boat and Albert threw on board his suitcase. As he prepared to follow the suitcase, a gust of wind swung the boat away from the shore so that the side of the boat on which he proposed to lever himself up had moved away and his arms were now at full stretch, with his lower limbs dangling in the water up to his waist. Kelp took some corrective action, the boat came back, and Albert was half-pulled, oozing, on board.

Kelp skilfully steered the boat into the river using the oars and for four or five hundred yards the boat raced with the fast-running river towards the Bay. As they entered the Bay they could see the Port Roger harbour installations and lights over to their left. Kelp felt it was safe to start up the outboard motor because he did not want to be at the mercy of currents now that they had entered the Bay and were virtually at sea. He also reckoned that the noise of the engine would hardly carry over the noise of the wind, and without lights they would soon be out of the Bay and round the headland.

Kelp pointed the boat towards the open sea and as they rounded the headland and the lights of Port Roger fell away from view, he opened the throttle. In daylight Kelp would have kept closer in to the shore for shelter, but in the dark he was concerned about running aground or, worse, striking submerged rocks which made the coastline something to be admired from a respectful distance. The sea itself was rarely calm and this night was no exception. As Kelp tried to keep a reasonable speed, the boat smacked into the waves, causing cascades of spray to be blown into the boat. For Albert it was too late to worry about getting wet. Only his braces were still dry, but even they would soon be sodden at this rate.

As Kelp had explained to Wentworth Stringer, the plan called for a coast-hugging sea journey of about 25 miles, so it was nearly three hours after embarkation when Kelp turned the boat shoreward and made for the mouth of a small river. The river turned at right angles close to its mouth and there, under an overhanging canopy of majestic trees, was a landing jetty. They were soon tied up alongside and Kelp was helping each of the MPs onto the jetty. Albert was very pleased indeed to feel stationary timber, as opposed to moving timber, under his feet — in so far as he could feel anything in any of his extremities. They set off from the jetty, following Kelp up a pathway towards a large, ranch-type house, whose lights beamed a welcome and the promise of warmth and hot water to come.

★ ★ ★

In the comfort and warmth of her room in Government House, Rosie Long was not sure how she felt. The part of her that was socialist still glowed with Heroic Resistancethe exhilaration of her earlier statement of principle, whereas the part of her which was a true Brit patriot had been hurt by Wentworth Stringer's letter and particularly the bit about her constituents with relatives in the Task Force. Britain would never risk lives to retake these God-forsaken islands — and in the year before an election, too. On the other hand ... She hesitated and then put the whole idea of a Task Force out of her mind.

Rose Catchpole had been twenty when she married Miners' Union activist Tom Long. He was hard-working, honest, faithful (as far as she knew) and never beat her. He also came from the north east Andy Capp culture, where a woman's place was firmly in the home. He had, however, been rather proud of her political progress and supported her until his sudden death five years previously.

Rosie and Tom had a marriage happy in the conventional sense, in that they did not row in public and they did try to understand and support each other. The one thing that no-one could accuse Tom Long of being, however, was soppy or romantic. He did not have a romantic thought in his being and as Rosie was a product of the same culture, her expectations were limited when it came to romance.

Rosie had found that she could cope with Tom's death because her sheer commitment to her political beliefs buoyed her up and kept her alert. She had not felt the need of an emotional prop or stimulus and if she had, it would have been unthinkable for such a person not to belong to the ranks of committed socialists.

Now an extraordinary set of circumstances had thrown her together with Luis Hernando, a General in the Marranesian Army. Whenever they had talked politics, the General had explained what his government wanted to do for his people and how everything was done in the name of the people. Rosie was not in any way a naive person, but of course she wanted to believe the words she heard. There was also no escaping the fact that the General was dark and handsome and, as with so many men, the uniform did him no harm. She saw in him a man of action who was trying to convert a shared political philosophy into action; she also saw someone who treated her with grace, consideration and charm, not qualities to which she had been over-exposed in recent years.

She thought about her three parliamentary colleagues, out there somewhere in the wind and rain, and she did not really feel sorry for them. They had brought this on themselves entirely. It was not as though they could do anything which was even remotely militarily significant. Wentworth Stringer was an overgrown Boy Scout reliving his wartime days and Rollo went along with him, and as for Albert Blackhead, what kind things could she find to say about Albert, she wondered? There was a pause while no kind thoughts came to her lips. Albert was easily led but, to be fair to him, he had always spoken out in favour of strong defence in the Parliamentary Labour Party meetings. The best she could hope for was that none of them would come to any harm. In any case, the Marranesian Army would find them tomorrow and they would be back in Government House in time for the flight out the following day.

The following morning General Hernando called to discuss the departure arrangements for those flying out.

Rosie Long was in the drawing room looking out at the well-manicured lawns, when the General's staff car drove in. The General entered the room and saluted.

'Good morning, Mrs Long.'

'Please call me Rosie.'

'Thank you, Rosie. I am Luis.'

'I know.'

The General stared at her for a moment and then asked, 'Is Mr Cunningham available? I wish to discuss arrangements for his flight.'

'I'll go and find him. Why don't you take a seat, Luis?' She smiled slightly nervously — almost as though she was a schoolgirl once again — and went in search of the former Governor. Mr Cunningham was in his study and he followed Rosie to the drawing room.

The General saluted Mr Cunningham and waited for him to sit down before resuming his seat. He then discussed the timings for the departure of the Cunninghams and Lord Hogshead and also the question of how much they would be able to take out on the plane in terms of their personal belongings.

'I will arrange for all of your possessions to be packed and sent to you in the UK, Mr Cunningham. Now that you will not be coming back.' Mr Cunningham flushed.

'I would prefer to wait and see, General.'

'As you wish, Mr Cunningham.'

'Have you seen my three other house guests, General?'

'Not as far as I am aware, but my men only began looking for them seriously this morning. There was some sort of disturbance in the town last night. They won't have gone far. In fact, I have hopes that they may rejoin us in time to take the flight out.'

'I would not count on that either, General.'

The General shrugged. 'Of course they can hide in a house in Port Roger for a few days but then ...' He spread his palms wide, as if to indicate the futility of the efforts of the three.

'Is your servant Kelp on duty, Mr Cunningham?'

'No, I sent him on indefinite leave. As I am going back to the UK with my wife, he needed time to think about whether the idea of working here for you appealed to him.'

'Where is his home?' asked the General sharply.

'Kelp lives here in the House. I believe he was born in Port Roger. He has relatives all over the Islands.'

'Rather a useful man to have along if one was going to go to ground in the Islands, wouldn't you think?'

'I wouldn't know about that.'

'No, I'm sure you wouldn't, Mr Cunningham.' The General decided to change tack. 'Mrs Long, I would ... Mrs Long I would like to invite you to inspect my Headquarters. Mr Cunningham, I will send the baggage party here at 10.00 hours tomorrow and transport for you and your wife and Lord Hogshead at 11.00 hours. I will, of course, accompany you to the aircraft myself.'

'You are too kind, General,' Mr Cunningham replied tartly. He had really had enough of all this Latin American charm, which he knew perfectly well was only skin-deep.

The General saluted and held open the door for Mrs Long. She got into the back seat of the car with the General and away they went, past the sentries and out of Government House. The seventy British Royal Marines had occupied a single storey building which now flew the Marranesian flag and was not very far from Government House. The Marines were still in the building unarmed and under guard, waiting to be flown out on the Cunningham flight the following day. The General had his Headquarters in the same office as that previously used by the Marine CO. He showed Rosie to a chair and ordered some coffee from the orderly.

'I wanted to get you away from that stifling atmosphere.'

'Thank you.'

'I have some good news for you. I have had a message from Defence Ministry Headquarters in Gazebo and they are very happy for you to stay, as long as you put out a statement to say that you are a complete volunteer. They are very sensitive that they might be accused of holding you against your will.'

'Do they know about the other three yet?'

'No, but I'll have to tell them. If I don't find them before the plane goes, then I will report them missing. It's a pity, but it's not the end of the world. In a way I quite admire them.'

Rosie frowned. 'And what do you think of me?'

'You are entirely different, Rosie. You are someone who is prepared to put her principles, and her political beliefs even, in front of the narrow national self-interest of her country. That is a super-patriotism, patriotism on an almost planetary scale. I have never encountered anything like it before, or anyone like you before.' He paused.

'I have some good news for you,' said Rosie. The General

waited, looking at Rosie as she received her coffee from the orderly.

'I will broadcast to the islanders for you. At noon and at six pm and on any special occasion. I will explain my commitment to them and to the Marxist Revolutionary cause. Wouldn't that be good?'

The General was delighted. 'It would be very good. An English voice speaking her native tongue. And someone with your great experience of working people. You can empathise with those who have been exploited for so long — the sheep farmers and fishermen. I think it is a wonderful idea and it is particularly wonderful because it is a matter within my operational control as Commander of our forces here. I can decide without reference to Gazebo. And I have decided.' Rosie beamed. 'This is wonderful, Rosie. We can develop something very special here.'

Rosie was not sure what the General had in mind, but she hoped it was not entirely about the Marxist Revolution. There was something about General Luis Hernando that made Rosie Long feel rather young again.

★ ★ ★

Wentworth Stringer cradled the glass of whisky in the palm of his hand and looked out to sea from the comfortable ranch-style home of sheep farmer Mulch. He and his colleagues were extremely grateful to the family Mulch. Thanks to them they had a new supply of sensible, reasonably well-fitting warm clothes and they had eaten and slept well. A Marranesian light aircraft had overflown the house in the morning and in the afternoon, but everyone had kept strictly indoors and there was no reason to suppose that any suspicions had been aroused. Mulch had no airstrip near him and the only boat visible at his jetty was his own, Kelp's boat having been hidden.

On their first day at the Mulch Mansion, Kelp had gone off in the Mulch boat to visit some of his friends and form a plan. The Marranesians would be looking from the air for three rather obvious Brits, not someone who was clearly a local, so it was worth the risk.

As darkness fell at the end of their first twenty-four hours of freedom, the three colleagues welcomed back Kelp and sat down at the Mulch dining table to plan their campaign. At the same time, in the Officers' Mess in Port Roger General Hernando — disappointed but not downhearted at having failed to locate the three — sat down to dinner with Rosie Long to plan a series of visits for her around the Islands to provide material for her radio broadcasts.

Wentworth Stringer said that the aim of their plan was simple. They had to become a nuisance to the occupying forces. They must disrupt their communications, tying up large numbers of troops in looking for them, troops that could be working on fortifications to resist the Task Force. The big prize, of course, would be the airfield, but they would not achieve anything unless they could capture automatic weapons and some radios for field operations. Kelp had identified an isolated Marranesian position at Huff Bay, sixteen miles further round the coast.

The plan would be to take the bigger Mulch boat with its two crew direct to Huff Bay at last light. Local boats went in there from time to time, so the Marranesians would not be immediately suspicious. Under cover of darkness the colleagues and Kelp would have to surprise and disarm a unit which Kelp understood to be of section strength, probably commanded by a Corporal. The main aim would be to seize weapons and ammunition and, of course, the radios. Already Wentworth Stringer was thinking ahead to the time when he and Rollo would have to split up and each be in charge of one of the two main islands. In the meantime, they made the most of the chance to rest in warm beds and consume nourishing food.

The following morning they were up early and Wentworth Stringer insisted that anyone wearing new boots — or rather, boots that were new to him — should spend a day in them to acclimatise. Both Albert and Rollo came in that category and they had been wriggling their toes in unfamiliar boots since tea-time the previous day. Shortly before twelve noon they gathered in the Mulch kitchen to hear the news summary. The main bulletins were at twelve noon and six in the evening. As Mulch turned on the radio, Lurk, the presenter-cum-announcer, was talking in between records and trying to sound as though this was just another day in the windswept history of the Faraway Islands.

'To carry us up to the twelve noon news bulletin, we have a message from Mr Alfred Doolittle, who wants you to know that he is getting married in the morning.'

Wentworth Stringer glanced at the faces in the kitchen. Rollo looked keen and alert, rather like a retriever awaiting its instructions. Albert, minus his trilby in the house, resembled a St Bernard which would get there in the end without being too sure what to do when it did get there. If Wentworth Stringer had looked in a canine mirror, he would have seen a whippet with a clipped military moustache looking back at him. In their various ways, they wondered what use would be made of such a powerful medium as the local radio now that the Islands had been overrun. They did not have to wait to find out.

'Pull out the stopper, let's have a whopper, and get me to the bloomin' church on time,' sang Stanley Holloway. The time signal for twelve noon sounded and then a woman's voice said, 'This is the news at twelve noon on Radio Free Faraway.' Everyone in the kitchen sat bolt upright. It was Rosie Long.

'This news bulletin is brought to you by Rosie Long MP. I have just returned from the airport, where I watched the departure of an aircraft carrying the former Governor of the Faraway Islands, Mr Cunningham, and his wife, Lord Hogshead of the British parliamentary delegation, the Commander of the British Royal Marines contingent here, and seventy-six Royal Marines. All of them are on their way home to the UK and they will not be coming back. Britain's rule finally ended when the aircraft took off and the long exploitation of the Faraway Islands people is over.

'Although I am a Member of the House of Commons and have been for many years, I felt it my duty not to desert the people of the Faraway Islands in their hour of need. I have therefore agreed to stay and to help the liberating forces of Marranesia as they commence their consolidation of the Islands and propose new instruments of government.

'General Luis Hernando, the Military Commander of the Islands, has summoned a meeting of the Islands' Executive Council for the day after tomorrow at eleven in the morning in

Government House. In the meantime, there is no curfew for the civilian population and it is hoped there will be only minimal disruption caused by the arrival of fresh troops to reinforce the garrison on the island.

'Each day large planes bring more troops and weapons to safeguard the integrity of your islands. The British will not try to retake them. They will bluster and talk big for a few days and then they will accept the inevitable.

'General Hernando and the Government of Marranesia which he represents guarantee your human rights and freedom of movement and welcome you all into fraternal union with the Marxist Republic of Marranesia. Your next bulletin will be at six o'clock this evening.'

Kelp turned off the radio and there was silence for a moment,.

Then Rollo banged his fist on the table. 'The cow!' he roared. 'What a traitor!'

'That tape will be a very powerful part of the case against her at the Old Bailey,' added Wentworth Stringer, almost sadly.

Albert shook his head very slowly and sighed as though he could hardly believe the evidence of his ears.

'Well, she's well and truly nailed her colours to the mast, so we had better start giving her some fresh news to report. Perhaps some news that she and her precious General were not expecting. I suggest we rest and take it easy this afternoon. Kit up and be ready to move at 18.00 hours.'

Wentworth Stringer was once again in command after allowing himself a few moments' genuine sadness about Rosie. However much he detested her politics, he had never disliked her as a person and he had always respected the sincerity of her beliefs. But this was too much.

As 18.00 hours approached, they assembled once more in the kitchen. Their faces were blackened and Wentworth Stringer and Rollo wore woollen hats. Albert insisted on his brown trilby crammed well down. They had two Mulch shotguns and Albert was armed only with a baseball bat. Kelp had his personal knife, which would be sufficient for close quarters work. They all now realised that the running war was over. They were now actively going to seek out the enemy. The objective was to seize weapons, radios and ammunition, and to be successful they would have to achieve total surprise. Their main intention was not to kill the enemy, but if necessary they would have to.

The previous day Wentworth Stringer had talked to them about the Marranesian Armed Forces, based broadly on what he had read over recent years and on accounts given him by his nephew, who was British Defence Attaché in Gazebo a few years ago.

He reminded his colleagues of the nature of the régime. It was not remotely benign. It systematically used torture on its opponents, many of whom simply disappeared. The Air Force was very professional and not very political, the Army the reverse. The crack elite units were very good, but overall the Army was full of conscripts, who were poorly educated country boys, lacking any form of *esprit de corps*. The officers and NCOs would have Marxist fanatics among them without doubt. The Navy was described as quite effective and fairly political, a sort of half-way house between the Air Force and Army.

On the morning of the raid, before the Rosie Long broadcast, Wentworth Stringer had gone over the raid on Huff Bay. He described the arrival of the Mulch boat with the two Mulch men visible and then the going ashore by the assault party and taking care of the first sentry. They would then have to seek out the main building to get at the weapons. Kelp had briefed them on the few phrases of Spanish they would need.

The Mulch boat was much more powerful than the boat they had used to escape from Port Roger and it was ten minutes after seven in the dusk when they saw the lights of the Huff Bay settlement. The crew kept the boat close to the coastline as long as possible to minimise the risk of a reception committee, but eventually they entered the small bay and made towards the only jetty.

Years later, when the stories were being written and films made, Albert was astonished to be told that the Huff Bay operation took 41 minutes from tie-up to cast-off. He would have been prepared to swear that the overall time was no more than 5 minutes and the reason he felt this was because of the sheer speed of Kelp and Wentworth Stringer.

Within what seemed like seconds, the first Marranesian sentry's unconscious body had flown off the jetty into the boat and the assault group was sprinting along the quay and up to the verandah and what looked like a general store. There were lights inside. Wentworth Stringer and Kelp kicked open the door and shouted in Spanish, 'British Commandos! Hands up!'

Seven pairs of Marranesian eyes looked at the blackened faces and the shotguns — and the knife. Surprise was total and terror absolute. Three of the conscripts, all teenagers, burst into tears and fell onto their knees. Kelp and Wentworth Stringer were looking for the NCO. The door to a side room opened at that moment and the Corporal came to see the cause of the noise. He was disarmed and tied by Rollo to the railings that ran around the side of the room.

Kelp told the soldiers to lift up the boxes of ammunition they had no doubt brought up from another boat only yesterday and take them in pairs to the Mulch boat. Rollo and Albert supervised the loading parties. Attention was then turned to the anti-tank rocket grenades, the AK47 automatic weapons and, most valuable of all, the Stinger surface-to-air missile-firing unit, complete with eight missiles. Only two radio sets were found and these too were loaded.

The Corporal began to scream and rage until Kelp slapped him and waved his knife in the direction of his genitals. The order was now given to withdraw. The unconscious sentry was thrown back onto the jetty. Just before cast-off, Wentworth Stringer used a paint spray, something he had always deplored and never thought to find himself using. On the wooden slats of the jetty he wrote -

TO RED ROSIE - HAVE A NICE DAY - BLUE FOX

The Mulch boat crew had rendered the only other boat at the jetty inoperable while the other work was being done. Without a shot being fired, the Mulch boat headed out to sea, the mission a total success. The only mishap had been Albert tripping over something on the jetty and vaulting into the water. The Mulch crew fished him out with ropes, minus the baseball bat but with the trilby.

It was a whole hour before the terrified conscripts were prepared to lift their faces from the prone position Wentworth Stringer and Kelp had ordered them to adopt on the jetty.

Eventually the curses and threats of their Corporal persuaded them that it was safe to move and they might indeed be in graver danger if they did not untie him.

With much trepidation the Corporal had to make his report over his military net to Headquarters in Port Roger. Whereas military experts might question whether British Commandos would really only be interested in seizing weapons and ammunition — if they were actually Commandos, that is — nonetheless the word was round the Marranesian forces in no time at all that such a force was active on the Islands. As the Marranesian officers had said that the British were not only capitalists but frequently cannibals as well, this piece of propaganda came back as something of a boomerang as far as the morale of the troops went.

Staff Officers decided that this piece of news could be given to the General the following morning. The General was dining alone with Rosie Long at Government House and had given orders not to be disturbed. The General's word was law in the Islands.

6

Heads Must Roll

♦

THE CHAIRMAN OF THE 22, as it is colloquially known, is a very influential figure in the Conservative Party. The present incumbent, Mr Cuthbert Smarm, had held the chairmanship for five years and saw himself as absolutely indispensable to the party, a view that was commanding less support as the months went by.

At the present moment, Smarm was at the centre of the stage and he knew it. After the preliminaries of the meeting were over, one of the joint secretaries opened the door and invited the Ministers in.

The Foreign Secretary was first into the room, followed by Lord Mafeking. They took seats to the right of the Chief Whip and faced the 1922 Committee. Not a sound had greeted their entry into the room.

Mr Smarm addressed the meeting. 'Foreign Secretary and Secretary of State for Defence, we are indeed grateful to you for kindly placing yourselves at the disposal of this Committee when you have such pressure on your time. I have urged the Committee to have regard to the duty that we all have to send our armed forces to meet the dangerous challenge of the unknown, confident in the knowledge that they have a united Conservative Party behind them.'

Lord Mafeking felt the start of a wave of nausea creeping up from his stomach. How could this awful man go on in this way when everyone had seen the real colours of the Tory Party in the House not an hour before?

There they sat, row after row of them, wets and dries, young blimps and old blimps, war veterans and never-fired-a-shot-in-anger veterans, saints, con men, adulterers, merchant bankers, lawyers, small businessmen, farmers, some very rich, some living on their parliamentary allowances and fiddling the expenses. Most of them were of poor or non-existent pedigree, from worse schools and with appalling wives, some of whom he had been forced to meet at Palace garden parties. There might not be much to be said for Lady Mafeking, but she did have pedigree and good breeding. These were the people the country had elected in 1979! Hardly any of them were good enough even to do up the Foreign Secretary's shoes and yet here they were, an only slightly genteel lynch mob.

The Foreign Secretary rose to his feet and spoke. The Committee heard the Foreign Secretary in silence and they greeted his speech respectfully, but not enthusiastically.

It was now Lord Mafeking's turn to speak. Some in the audience thought him a decent enough old stick and two of them had actually fagged for him at Eton, but they were hardly in a majority. The older ones who took an interest in defence regarded highly his war record, but doubted its relevance to modern technology, and the younger ones who followed defence were convinced that he belonged with the Zeppelin in the Imperial War Museum.

'Mr Smarm,' he boomed. 'It is a rare privilege for a Member of the other place to be allowed to address this committee, although I and you would wish that we had different circumstances for bringing us together.'

Mafeking had wisely (on Sergeant Banger's advice) concentrated on what was to be done, rather than looking back to how the government had got itself into the mess. This gained him support. The banging on the desk tops was quite supportive in both depth and duration, in contrast to the perfunctory response to the Foreign Secretary.

Tom Scintilla had left the room during Smarm's closing remarks and soon came hurrying back. He placed a note in front of Smarm, who had to put on his spectacles to read it.

'It may be for the convenience of the Committee if I were to tell you that Mr Scintilla has just handed me a tape recording which has been made in the past hour of a broadcast received from the Faraway Islands. With your permission, this tape will now be played on the tape recorder.'

Scintilla reached across in front of Smarm, who had resumed his seat at the centre of the raised platform facing the rows and rows of flushed and expectant faces, and inserted the tape into the recorder and pressed the start button. There was a pause and then the unmistakable voice of their colleague, Wentworth Stringer. The silence throughout Committee Room 14 was extraordinary, as though everyone was holding their breath.

'This is Wentworth Stringer, Member of the House of Commons, speaking to you from the British Faraway Islands. As you know, the Faraway Islands have been invaded and seized by Marranesian forces. The parliamentary delegation has effectively been under house arrest in the former Government House. The plan of the Marranesian Commander, General Hernando, was to fly out all the Brits, that is to say, the Governor, our delegation and the Royal Marine contingent, who gave such an admirable account of themselves before they were overwhelmed by superior numbers.

'Our delegation debated this situation among themselves in the best tradition of British democracy. Some of us decided to slip away from Government House and join the local people and help the resistance. The leader of our delegation, Rosie Long, takes the very opposite view. She wishes to stay and give her full support to the Marxist invaders. She will be judged by history and the British people.

'George Hogshead would like to come with us but is not up to it physically, and will soon be back in the UK with the rest of the party. Rollo Herbert-Fitzherbert and Albert Blackhead are with me. We are all in good spirits, but conditions are difficult — very wet and windy, and we can only move at night.

'We aim to cause a few problems for the Marranesians before the Task Force gets here. We send our very best wishes to all our friends and to peace- loving people everywhere. God save the Queen.'

As the tape stopped there was thunderous applause in the form of more banging on desk tops. Several members dabbed at the corners of their eyes as the emotion of Wentworth Stringer's message got through to them. It was an unprecedented moment in the history of the 1922 Committee.

★ ★ ★

Banger drove along Millbank and turned to cross Lambeth Bridge. The weather had deteriorated and it was quite cold for early April. A stiff breeze was flapping the trousers of a group of Chinese or Japanese who were gathered in a clump round two of their number who were taking photographs of Big Ben from Lambeth Bridge. Banger pointed the car towards the Old Kent Road and opened conversation with His Lordship. The journeys were never quite long enough to get through the affairs of state which he had to encourage Lord Mafeking to discuss. Some of the time was wasted in drawing details out of His Lordship because some pretending was necessary. Though Banger already had all the information that he needed, he could not be too blatant about it; even Lord Mafeking could get offended.

'How did the 1922 Committee meeting go, Me Lord?' began Banger after he had squeezed the bulb of the little klaxon horn which he had fitted below the fascia board. In the days when klaxons were used they were fitted externally to motor cars, but Banger had obtained one for internal use. He had persuaded Lord Mafeking that because of His Lordship's hearing impediment, it was important that Banger should attract his attention first by sounding the klaxon should he have something to say. The klaxon always nearly shot Lord Mafeking off the seat, but it worked because he was fully ready, if irritable, for Banger's words when they came.

'Well, the best that could be said was that the Foreign Secretary and I got out alive, if only just.' He paused and then added, 'Actually, I think my piece went down reasonably well.'

'That's very good, Me Lord. It must have been a very difficult meeting.'

Lord Mafeking looked pleased in the back seat. Banger knew full well how the meeting had gone even though the *cosa nostra* of the government car service had had very limited time for drivers to debrief their respective bosses and then activate the drivers' network.

'I gather things don't look good for the Foreign Secretary.' There was no point in Banger continually pretending that all these views were his own. It did no harm to acknowledge occasionally that a certain amount of gathering had been done.

'You gather correctly,' replied Lord Mafeking.

'How soon do you think before he puts in his resignation?' Banger was getting blunter because they were already at New Cross and he did not want to risk taking His Lordship on a roundabout route in case he noticed.

'I should think he is probably writing it at this very moment,' replied Lord Mafeking with commendable frankness.

Banger took a deep breath. 'Have you considered your own position, Me Lord?' There was silence from the back seat.

'Well ... er ... not completely. I did not get the impression from the parliamentary party that they were expecting that sort of gesture from me.'

'I think you're absolutely right, Me Lord, but you should consider whether because of that very reason, this might not be a very good moment to offer your resignation.'

'But what happens if the Prime Minister accepts my resignation? After all, we're not exactly close friends.'

'That's a risk we'll ... er ... you'll have to take, Me Lord, but if the Foreign Secretary is going to resign, the Prime Minister will have no alternative but to accept his resignation. What the Prime Minister does not want is to lose her Defence Secretary as well at the very moment that the fleet are getting ready to sail. What I'm concerned about, me Lord, is that the Foreign Office really want to stitch you up over this Faraways business. They wanted it before their Foreign Minister resigns and they're going to want it with bells on now. The same officials who worked for the old Foreign Secretary will work for the new one. If their man was going to have to go — and they have accepted that that's inevitable — they want to try and send you off to the knackers' yard with him.'

'Steady on, Banger, I don't think that is the way to speak of the Foreign Secretary or even myself.'

'I'm sorry, Sir. It's just that I don't like to see these people putting one over on you. You are vulnerable over HMS *Reluctance* and the playing down of the signals from her Captain, but this is not enough for any Prime Minister to expect you to resign.'

'That's what I thought I said.'

'Yes, Me Lord, you did and I agree with you. It means that it is very, very unlikely that the Prime Minister would accept your offer of resignation.'

'Oh good,' said Lord Mafeking, as though that was the end of the matter.

Banger, however, thought differently. 'The point I was getting at, Me Lord,' and he summoned up every ounce of patience, 'was if you offer your resignation and the Prime Minister refuses to accept it, your position in the government is much stronger. The Prime Minister has refused to let you go. You have been confirmed in office: it's as good as a vote of confidence. After that, it's going to be really hard for those poofters in the Foreign Office to stitch you up.'

Banger negotiated a major intersection with the South Circular Road and listened to Lord Mafeking thinking behind him. It was a painful process, but by keeping to the inside lane on a piece of dual carriageway, he bought some time and after a mile or two Lord Mafeking had decided more or less.

'I can see what you're driving at, Banger. Jolly clever scheme.' Then the return of doubts.

'But what will I put in the — much will turn on how I phrase — I mean I can't just toss in a couple of lines to the Prime Minister, now can I?'

Banger was now reeling in the line with Lord Mafeking well and truly hooked. 'On the seat beside you, Me Lord, in the buff envelope you will find a draft of your resignation letter. It uses lots of your usual phrases.'

Lord Mafeking took out the letter from the unsealed buff envelope and read it slowly. The light was so poor, even in the middle of the day, that he had to put on the reading light which shone from a small light fitting over his right ear.

'Neither Brian nor Jolyon knows about this, Me Lord. This would be something between us here in the car.' Banger knew this would please His Lordship, and probably answered his last remaining question.

' "I therefore feel that I must place my resignation in your hands, offering you my continued support in the difficult tasks" — this is a bit flowery, isn't it?' asked his Lordship.

'I've taken phrases from resignation letters in the past. They're all in the memoirs, Harold Macmillan and all that.'

'I suppose it's all right. But how do people know I've put it in?'

'No way will they be able to keep this a secret. The Lord Privy Seal is in charge of government communications and his driver and me have arranged to see the Chief Press Officer's driver — he's a junior chap and there'll be no problem there.'

'Have arranged?' Lord Mafeking was slightly quizzical.

'Er... subject to your Lordship's approval and consent, of course,' gushed Banger, as the gates of the former rectory that Lord Mafeking called home came into view. 'If you agree the draft and would care to sign it, Me Lord, I can deliver it within the hour to Number Ten.'

Without another word Lord Mafeking re-read the letter and topped and tailed it with a flourish. He handed it to Banger and let himself into his front door. The mystical union between Minister and driver was preserved and strengthened.

7

A New Foreign Secretary

♦

IT WAS NEARLY MIDNIGHT when the Prime Minister telephoned. Lord Mafeking had just had a bath and had gone downstairs, wearing only his slippers, to pour himself a nightcap. When he realised it was the Prime Minister, he asked her to wait and quickly put on a velvet smoking jacket and adjusted his hearing aid. As far as he knew the Prime Minister could not yet see down a telephone, but those scientific chappies were always beavering away and if anyone would be the first to demonstrate it, it would be Herself. Better be on the safe side.

Lord Mafeking was told that his resignation could not be accepted — although it might be on some other occasion. Nonetheless Lord Mafeking got the clear impression of a distinct, if grudging, tone of admiration for the position he had taken. He was gratified by that because it enabled him to show that he had some political flair. He was not to be regarded as one of the last remaining examples of a virtually extinct species — the Political Booby.

He was told that the Foreign Secretary had submitted his resignation and attempts were being made to dissuade him, but he was proving adamant. An announcement would be made the following day, probably about lunchtime. He would be told before the public announcement. The Prime Minister rang off.

Every Sunday paper featured the Foreign Secretary's resignation, together with pictures, background analysis and speculation about his successor. All the heavies carried Lord Mafeking's photograph — a half-asleep snap taken while listening to the defence debate at the previous year's Party Conference and which he had tried to have suppressed — together with news of his proffered resignation. There was favourable comment on both his gesture and the Prime Minister's reaction to it.

At the breakfast table Lady Mafeking screeched and said various things. He motioned to the newspapers so that she should have an inkling that something was going on. She caught sight of his unflattering photograph and emitted what appeared to be a low whooping sound, followed by some uncatchable comments. She was beginning to eye the buttered toast with a faraway look. Lord Mafeking thought it might be wise if he withdrew to the study and this he did, leaving the tabloid horror comics, as he called them, with his wife.

Once safe in his study, he continued his perusal of the Sunday heavies. The favourite choice to be the new Foreign Secretary was Roger Woodcock, at present a Minister of State at the Department of Industry. Other people were mentioned, but the clear consensus on the part of the political commentators was for Woodcock. The outgoing Foreign Secretary was a man whom Lord Mafeking respected, admired and liked. Roger Woodcock was someone for whom he could feel none of these things.

When Lord Mafeking thought back to the snarling faces in the 1922 Committee the previous day, he was hard pressed to think of anyone who more completely encompassed all in the party that he most detested than Roger Woodcock. For a start, he was self-made and both pushy and insecure, as these people so often were. He came from somewhere in the west country, went to a strict grammar school, got a scholarship to Oxford, was President of the Union and a soccer blue and afterwards made a lot of money in property back in the west country, having also been prudent enough to marry the only daughter of a local supermarket millionaire.

In appearance Woodcock was above average height, but not unusually tall; he had dark, sleek, almost 1920s, hair, expressive hands, which he used a lot to accentuate and punctuate his conversation, and a face which was almost classically handsome. His mouth, however, was weak and his smile, which was ready and frequent enough, seemed a nervous smile. His voice was firm and well modulated, with no trace of any west country accent. No-one knew what contact, if any, he maintained with his original family and, indeed, whether or not his father, who had retired early as a lorry driver, was still alive.

Woodcock had leapt to national prominence when he was

called on at short notice to deputise at the Party Conference the previous year for the Secretary of State for Industry, and he seized this opportunity with both hands and delivered a barnstorming speech which delighted the party faithful. After that he was at the top of every list of desirable speakers and the lady at Central Office whose job it was to arrange speakers was overwhelmed with constituency associations writing and telephoning and all seeking an early date — or any date — for Roger Woodcock to come and address their annual general meeting or divisional ball or political supper.

Although there were some who were unmoved, it was the women with whom Woodcock made his greatest hit. He was reputed to be able to charm not only the birds from the trees, but also the pants from the birds once down from the trees. The Prime Minister was reported to look favourably on this relative newcomer although, of course, her pants were distinctly not for charming.

Woodcock had entered the House at a by-election in 1972 and his rise since then had indeed been rapid. Inevitably he had detractors who envied his success. He was described by these people as being superficial and lacking in any intellectual depth. His speeches were criticised for being too full of clichés and colourful phrases, but his critics would have given their eye teeth to have received the plaudits that Woodcock received from his audiences. He had charisma and if he was promoted to the office of Foreign Secretary, he would have arrived as a major, if undeclared, contender for the succession to the leadership after Herself.

Roger Woodcock was telephoned by one of the Prime Minister's Private Secretaries late on Saturday evening and asked if he could see the Prime Minister at four o'clock the next afternoon.

He drove himself to Downing Street and had to explain who he was to the policeman on duty at the barrier at the end of the street. He was obviously not yet well enough known. That was about to change, he felt confidently.

The policeman at the famous black door seemed to know who he was and tapped smartly for the door to be opened. Inside Paul Newton, the Private Secretary, was waiting to conduct Roger

Woodcock to the Prime Minister's study. In the entrance hall Woodcock felt the white marble chequered floor under his feet as he set off down the long corridor with high windows on his right and portraits of actors and actresses on his left.

Although he had been to Number Ten many times before — whether for receptions, or dinners, or informal meetings, or Cabinet committee meetings which were often attended by Ministers of lower than Cabinet rank — this was the most auspicious visit he had ever made. At least, he hoped it was. Whenever the Prime Minister decided to change her government team, various individuals were invited to call on her. Those not already in the government could be reasonably confident of a satisfactory outcome because it was unlikely that the Prime Minister would ask them in to tell them that she had not got a job to offer them.

It was those already in the government who could approach such an appointment with mixed feelings. They might be promoted, but they could just as easily be moved sideways or sacked altogether. It is by no means uncommon for Ministers to tread the gold-coloured carpets with a spring of anticipation in their step, only to emerge minutes later as ex-Ministers. One Minister had even been invited to Chequers on a Sunday, but instead of a strategy discussion he had been moved, and to a less senior post.

Roger Woodcock had devoured years before all the political biographies he could, but his favourite story of this type of situation was of the Labour Minister sacked by Clem Attlee, who asked why he had been given the push. Attlee, never a lover of long speeches, had simply replied, 'No good.'

The Prime Minister was waiting for him in her study. 'Come in, Roger.'

The convention decreed use of Christian names between colleagues except when speaking to the Prime Minister, who would be addressed by the office except for by some very close friends.

Woodcock glanced at the striking portrait of the young Nelson before sitting down. Here he was at the very hub of power, the holy of holies. The Prime Mininister had stamped her personality on the room, from the cream-coloured damask furniture to the neat grey striped wallpaper. He suspected that she probably liked him more than he liked her. As a self-made achiever, he was very much the stereotype of her 'make it happen' type of person.

She was looking at him.

'Roger, we're going to have to make some changes because of the Faraway Islands situation. I want you to be Foreign Secretary.'

Roger tried to check an almost involuntary desire to punch the air in triumph or to embrace Her in ecstasy. The last would definitely not have been appreciated and could have caused the Prime Minister to have second thoughts.

'Thank you very much for your confidence. It's going to be a very difficult assignment,' he heard himself saying. What on earth does one say on such occasions? he thought. She was speaking.

'The Cabinet Committee OD (SP) will meet tomorrow at eleven. Before that we will have a meeting of a smaller group, which will include you. That will meet at ten. I think you will have some reading to do tonight. I want to put out the announcement about you at five o'clock so that we will get the evening newscasts.'

There was a pause and Woodcock realised that the interview was over apart from the small talk. He made to excuse himself and the Prime Minister rose. Before permitting him to leave, she showed him the Queen Anne walnut bureau, which stood impressively in one corner of the study. As they were about to part in the doorway, the Prime Minister suddenly adopted a confidential tone. 'How is that nice wife of yours?'

'Very well indeed, thank you, Prime Minister.'

'Oh good. Hinton St George is such a charming village, I always think.'

'Yes, yes, indeed it is.'

It was now time to be escorted along the corridor and congratulated by the Private Secretary. Television cameras were outside, recording any arrivals and departures. The lights were switched on as Woodcock emerged, but he waved aside the shouted questions by saying that an announcement would be made later. As he drove himself away, the Prime Minister's question about Hinton St George nagged in his mind. 'Is there anything that woman doesn't know?' he asked himself and went to his Pimlico home to do some telephoning.

Shortly before ten the following morning a group which rapidly became known as the War Cabinet assembled in the anteroom outside the Cabinet Room at Number Ten. Roger Woodcock had made sure he was there a good ten minutes early, waving cheerfully to the cameras as he entered. Then the others arrived, each congratulating him with what seemed genuine warmth, but was not. Instead of welcoming an addition to their ranks (and one with presentational ability) at a time of crisis for the government, they could only see his appointment in terms of how much of a threat it would be to their own positions. Woodcock was reminded of the old adage about a man stepping forward and greeting a friend and rival warmly by the throat. He had considerable disdain for this jealousy, for that was all it was, and he did not hold his fellow War Cabinet colleagues in particularly high regard.

The one exception was the Chairman of the Party, Brendan Brilliant, who would probably emerge as Woodcock's main rival for the leadership once the great She Elephant had passed through the gates of the Carlton Club into the everlasting hall of fame. Brilliant was perfectly cast for his job in one important particular and this was that he was adored by the party faithful. He was standing ovation material each year at whichever seaside watering hole was hosting the Party Conference. Each year they roared with his rhetoric, his annihilation of Labour and its Militant Tendency, and his ridicule of the Alliance with its gaps as wide as a chasm. Every year Brilliant would toss his mane of red hair and as it became progressively dishevelled, a thousand Tory matrons stretched forth their hands to render assistance.

Not a man to take lightly as a rival for the top job, but not someone who devoured work. Where Woodcock would devour a brief and quote from it, Brilliant would tend to fly sight-unseen with his brief just opened in front of him. His aversion to detail and the minutiae of party organisational matters made him a less than ideal Chairman, rather than some less flamboyant but more practical figure. No such rival had come forward, so Brilliant was probably secure in his post until after the next election was safely won.

The others in the War Cabinet were the Leader of the House of Commons, the Chief Whip, and of course the Secretary of

State for Defence and the Chief of the Defence Staff. The Leader of the House, Tommy Tunstall, was very tall, oozed bonhomie and emollience and appeared to sleep in his Brigade of Guards tie. The Chief Whip, William Hopper, was short, dark and watchful, a modern Citizen Chauvelin, the eyes very small and pig-like. Woodcock represented the new radical meritocratic movement in the Tory Party and as such he resented the eminence of such pillars of the establishment as Tunstall and Hopper, whose talents were so manifestly less than his own. He well knew that they patronised him and his type and cackled with mirth about the meritocrats over glasses of port at Whites or Pratts, their London clubs.

Tunstall and Hopper were as Nobel prize-winners when compared to Arthur Mafeking, in the estimation of Woodcock. Woodcock had the meritocrat's contempt for the House of Lords and his contempt was confirmed by the quality of those Peers who were selected as Ministers. Woodcock had only met Lord Mafeking on three previous occasions, but it had been hate at first sight. No trace of rivalry here for future advancement, only a complete lack of respect for inherited position.

Arthur Mafeking had with him an upright figure in naval uniform, who was introduced as Admiral Sir Trimmer Halliard, the Chief of the Defence Staff. To Woodcock, Sir Trimmer appeared the very picture of a modern naval gentleman and if Woodcock was honest with himself, he would have admitted that Service people made him feel ill at ease. This was probably due to his own lack of military experience, which should not matter in this day and age, but still seemed to do so in the patrician circles of the party.

Tunstall was the last to arrive, bustling along the corridor from the front door and carrying his red box.

'Congratulations, Roger, this is very good news,' he said, shaking hands. 'More co-operation needed between Lords and Commons,' Tunstall went on, feeling that a statement of the obvious was needed.

'That's no problem for the Ministry of Defence,' said Roger Woodcock confidently. 'As long as we can be sure that they have graduated onto joined up writing and can understand our signals.'

'At least we know whose side we're on,' remarked Arthur

Mafeking dryly. He had responded quickly to Roger Woodcock's sarcasm, the tone of which he recognised at once, even if he was less clear about the joined up writing allusion.

'Whatever happens, we must avoid making ourselves look foolish in the eyes of the world,' said Woodcock quietly.

'We have first to face the fact that we already, now, this moment ...' said Tunstall, and to emphasise his point jabbed his finger down onto his red box, which he had put on the brown baize table, 'already look totally foolish in the eyes of the country.'

'And that includes the Party,' said Brilliant.

'I think, Roger, as the Foreign Office is somewhat under a cloud on this affair, it might be as well to play the matter cautiously. It is not the moment to apportion blame — yet,' said the Chief Whip.

The Prime Minister appeared from the direction of her study with her Principal Private Secretary, Sir Philip Prolix. The doors of the Cabinet Room were opened by an attendant and the War Cabinet was about to hold its first session.

8

Enemy Intelligence

◆

TO THE GENERAL Rosie was an object of utter fascination. For a start, he had had virtually no experience of politicians, who in his country were either murderous ex-military men of Marxist or Fascist persuasion or an occasional pathetic democrat involuntarily lodging at police headquarters. He had read about British politics but never thought he would meet an actual live British politician, let alone a woman politician, let alone a woman politician who clearly and passionately believed in her political faith. He was determined to try to weave his spell over her and so far had no reason to believe he would be rejected.

He was delighted with her offer to help with broadcasts to the islanders and he had reported how well her first broadcast had gone when he communicated with HQ in Gazebo. This had helped to ease the irritation felt by Gazebo at the defection of the three MPs. The General remained confident that the three MPs would soon be found, but he had been surprised by their defection. In fact he was somewhat taken aback by all of them.

Here was Rosie, remarkable, reasonable, passionate Rosie, who wanted to stay on the Islands and help the solidarity of the international working class. Then from the same party came Albert Blackhead, who had neither stayed with Rosie nor gone back to the UK, but had run off on a madcap scheme to join up with the islanders — if he could find any islanders who wanted or could be bothered to join him in anything. The islanders did not know much, but they did guess that the British Foreign Office would like to get shot of them. They knew for certain that they had had very little investment or expenditure from the British Government over the years. On top of that, they were, after decades of inbreeding, somewhat slow and apathetic. With a backdrop of wind and rain, this was not the tinder-dry scenario for the forest fire of political revolution. And yet Albert Blackhead had gone and done it.

Even the two Tory MPs had surprised the General, not so much by their attitude but by the hopelessness of their cause. Why go on when you cannot possibly win? The General was still annoyed. Nonetheless he was responsible for the welfare of the MPs and for finding them and getting them safely repatriated as soon as possible. It was the one blot on an otherwise impeccable invasion operation.

Rosie and the General had abandoned pretences and had shared the Cunninghams' double bed. The General decided that it was more romantic to have breakfast in the private sitting room adjoining their bedroom and Rosie heard the cups and saucers rattling as the breakfast tray was put in place behind the double doors.

'Did you sleep well, Rosie?' the General asked.

'Oh yes, very well thank you.'

'I think I heard breakfast arriving.' The General crossed the bedroom and opened the double doors into the sitting room to reveal the breakfast table set with two chairs facing each other at the table.

'Come through when you are ready. Would you like some coffee?'

'Yes please,' replied Rosie, putting on a quilted housecoat over her nightdress. The General poured the coffee and proffered the orange juice and rolls.

'I know you like a good English fried breakfast,' he said. Rosie agreed and almost on cue the orderly entered with a tray containing her fried eggs and bacon, some more coffee and a message for the General. Rosie prepared to attack the eggs and bacon while the General read the message. The orderly waited to see if the General wanted to send a reply, but the General shook his head and waved the man away. Rosie cut into her egg and watched the yolk collapse on the plate. The General had said nothing.

'Well?' said Rosie.

'It seems we have found your three colleagues,' said the General in measured tones.

Rosie was alarmed. 'Are they all right?' she asked sharply.

'They seemed in very rude health — when last seen,' replied the General slightly testily.

'I don't understand you, Luis. There's something you're not telling me. What is it?'

The General paused. 'When I said we have found your three colleagues, that was in one sense a statement of fact but it was still inaccurate. The absolute truth is that your three colleagues have found us. Our section position at Huff Bay was attacked at last light yesterday evening by a group of four men claiming to be British Commandos. They were brought to Huff Bay in a large motor boat with a crew of two or three. They achieved total surprise, disarmed the section and made off with a quantity of arms and ammunition. No-one was injured in the attack. That would appear to be the English translation of this message.' The General indicated the paper which he held between his finger and thumb.

Rosie felt a return of the mixed feelings that she had felt when the invasion had just taken place. She remained totally supportive of the Marranesians and their invasion but she worried about her colleagues too. Surely they would have to stop these games? Next time they might not achieve surprise. Marranesians would fire at them. They could well be killed. She twisted her napkin on her lap. If only they would get stuck in a bog, be rescued by the Army, brought back here safely and flown back to the UK to live happily ever after, all would be well. But all wasn't going to be well, she knew it. The General was looking at her intently. Rosie decided to take the initiative.

'I shall include this incident in my twelve noon bulletin.'

'You most certainly will not.'

'Of course I will.'

'No, absolutely not.' The General was emphatic. 'I do not want to disturb the population with such a trivial story.' He now sounded conciliatory.

'If it is such a trivial story, what's wrong with my broadcasting it?' flashed back Rosie.

'Because it gives some aid and comfort to the enemy.'

'So you agree this action is of some military significance, then? Don't you see, Luis, you can't have it both ways? Either the raid is very trivial indeed, in which case we can laugh at it and treat it in that way, or it is really quite serious. In either case, if you want to have people on your side you must explain what is going on and put your case. Wentworth Stringer is no fool and he will be broadcasting his exploits all over the Islands.'

She stared at him. He shrugged.

'I cannot allow you to broadcast about this, he said.

Rosie was upset. 'Let me explain why I am upset,' she said. 'What really bothers me is what this tells me about your attitude to the people of the Islands. You are their liberator from capitalist domination and exploitation, but you are not prepared to tell them the truth. It's crazy.' She subsided and pushed away her plate of now congealed egg and bacon. The General stood up and came round behind Rosie's chair and put his hands on her shoulders.

'You are a politician and I am not. Your political judgment is excellent. I am a soldier and I make a military judgment because I have to think about my men and what they are thinking. Let me make a suggestion. Let us get dressed and I will arrange for you and me to fly by helicopter to Huff Bay and see for ourselves. We can talk to the men on the ground and we can both think about our positions, although I am bound to say I don't see myself changing my mind just yet. But then, if anyone could persuade me you could.'

Rosie kissed his hand and went to get dressed.

★★★

Wentworth Stringer had already sent one tape back to the UK via George Hogshead, but he valued above all the opportunity to broadcast to the islanders, because he wanted them to know that there was a British-run resistance operating on the Islands. That said, Wentworth Stringer was a sufficient realist to know that he was not operating in World War II France or Yugoslavia with well-armed and determined maquis or partisans working with him on the ground. It was not unusual for an islander to be eighty or a hundred miles away from his nearest neighbour, which made co-ordinated local action very difficult, but it was highly beneficial that the islanders knew what was going on.

The other aspect of broadcasting which was in the mind of Wentworth Stringer was the damage he could do to the morale of the Marranesian forces by the reports of his group's Scarlet Pimpernel activities. Having seen now at first hand at Huff Bay the quality of some of the occupying forces, he reckoned that there was a good target to be hit, providing broadcasts could be made in Spanish. Rollo had done Spanish at Cambridge and had taken up a phrase book and cassette at the Mulch Mansion to start to get himself back up to speed. He had already discussed with Wentworth Stringer a plan which would involve the two of them separating and running operations from each of the two big islands, with Rollo broadcasting in Spanish and Wentworth Stringer broadcasting in English.

Wentworth Stringer sat in front of the microphone in the Mulch Mansion. This would be a historic broadcast because it would be his first since the Royal Marine garrison had left. He had written out his address.

> *'People of the Faraway Islands. A resistance unit has been established on the Islands under my command. Last night, shortly after 7 o'clock, a raiding party went ashore and attacked the Marranesian unit at Huff Bay. The Marranesian unit surrendered without offering resistance and their weapons and ammunition were removed. There were no casualties on either side and the raiding party withdrew in good order.*
>
> *'The Marranesian forces are here on the Islands as an occupying force. Until British forces arrive to throw them off— as they will— none of us on the Islands must assist them in any way. I am asking you not to provide any goods or services to the Marranesian forces. We will mount more attacks on the Marranesians. On no part of the Islands will they feel safe. You cannot contact me, but I will be contacting you through my call-sign, Blue Fox. God Save the Queen.'*

Wentworth Stringer switched off the microphone and then he and Kelp disconnected the short-wave radio and carried it outside and down the steps to the Mulch boat where the rest of the group was already on board. He was keen to get away from Mulch Mansion quickly before the Marranesians got their direction-finding equipment working and deduced where he was. He did not want to make extra trouble for Executive Council Member Mulch, who had been very kind and supportive to them. Kelp already had another safe haven in mind as the Mulch boat headed out to sea with Kelp's cousin's boat towed behind, as the Mulch boat would come back to the Mansion once they were safely dropped.

★ ★ ★

Rosie had never been in a helicopter before. She had thoughtfully worn a brown trouser suit, which certainly proved to be easier for getting up into the Puma helicopter than a tight skirt would have been. The General was at her elbow supervising the adjustment of her straps and buckles as the crew — all helmet, microphone and flak jacket — busied themselves for take-off.

Rosie heard the engine revolutions increase and the throaty roar grow more intense. After brief gyrations and shudderings, the aircraft was clearly airborne and the General had placed a reassuring hand on her hand. Rosie was sitting facing the open exit door, so she and the General had a good view of Government House and the roofs of Port Roger before the helicopter turned west and headed at around eight hundred feet for Huff Bay.

After about thirty minutes, they were over Huff Bay and Rosie could see uniformed figures running about on the main jetty. They seemed to be placing what looked like empty sacks on the jetty. The helicopter *H* landing pad in a field was a few hundred yards above Huff bay itself. The helicopter circled the landing area and, the pilot having satisfied himself that there were no obstructions such as trees or power cables, the landing took place slowly and carefully. They waited on board until the engines were switched off. Unless there were operational reasons for a rapid, engines-running exit, the General always preferred a dignified exit from a helicopter rather than trying to hold onto his hat in the updraft and salute at the same time.

The rotor blades slowed and the General helped Rosie from the helicopter. He then turned to face the Corporal, who had halted about twenty paces from him and who had been able to replace his hat once the helicopter's engine had closed down. Also on the Puma were the General's Chief of Staff, Colonel Olio, and some other junior ranks.

The General moved forward unsmiling. The Corporal saluted. 'Corporal Gomez, Sir. Eight men at their place for your inspection, Sir.'

'Corporal Gomez, you had better show us on the ground what happened. My Chief of Staff will take notes.'

The General and his Chief of Staff exchanged glances and the party walked across the field, which was wet as Faraway fields always were, and then down a gentle grassy slope to the Huff Bay settlement.

In front of the settlement shop Corporal Gomez had his section drawn up in a line. He brought them to attention and accompanied the General along the line. Rosie was following four or five paces behind with one of the General's English-speaking ADCs accompanying her to translate. She could not hear what the General was saying or any of the replies. Presently the General concluded his inspection of the line and wheeled round to tell the Corporal to continue the conducted tour. The General also indicated with a wave of his hand and his first Huff Bay smile that Rosie could talk to the men or do anything else that she would like to do.

The General plus entourage and Corporal Gomez moved off in the direction of the jetty to look at the damaged boat and the place where the assailants came ashore. Rosie suggested that she and the men might like to go into the shop and find some seats, which they did.

Rosie sat in a chair, with the men in an olive green semi-circle around her and the ADC next to her. They all looked impossibly young.

'How old are you?' she asked the nearest one. 'Eighteen,' came the reply in translation, and so on round the group. There was one twenty year old veteran.

'Do you know why you are here?' Rosie asked.

'The Islands belong to Marranesia. We came to take them back,' answered the round-faced boy opposite her.

'Did you come in the helicopter?' asked the same boy.

'Yes. With General Hernando.' Rosie couldn't be sure, but

she thought she felt a frisson of alarm at the very mention of the General's name.

'Can you describe the men who carried out the raid yesterday?'

They all thought for a few moments. The same boy again, 'They had black faces, but one of them was quite fat and wore a strange brown hat ...' That's Albert, thought Rosie. 'He carried a baseball bat and whacked some of us on the legs when we were carrying ammunition to their boat.'

'Did he indeed?' One for the notebook, thought Rosie.

The young soldiers, while clearly terrified of the General, seemed to have welcomed a chat with Rosie, something of a mother-figure in terms of age. Rosie indicated that they should probably go back outside and perhaps they had duties to resume.

The General, his Chief-of-Staff, and some others who had been on the helicopter, were talking together on the jetty. Of the hapless Corporal Gomez there was no sign. When the General caught sight of Rosie he waved, dismissed his group and hurried to her side.

'How were my young men?' he asked.

'Very young. Very young indeed,' she replied.

'Yes. They are good boys. It is their leader who must not let them down.' He paused for a moment. 'Shall we go back to Government House for coffee and give you time to prepare your broadcast? I think we have seen everything we need to see here.'

'There's just one thing I'd like to look at,' smiled Rosie, 'on the jetty.' They walked over to the jetty.

'As we were arriving I saw men putting what looked like empty sacks down here. Yes, here they are.' She began lifting them up and as she did so large letters of graffiti came into view.

'All right,' said the General. 'Let's see what it says.'

The group stared down at the jetty at their feet. There, in large white letters were the words:

TO RED ROSIE - HAVE A NICE DAY - BLUE FOX.

Despite herself Rosie blushed. The General said nothing.

The party retraced their steps up the slope from the bay to the helicopter pad where the Puma awaited. Rosie couldn't help noticing that it was another Corporal who saluted and bade the

General goodbye. As the Puma rose and swung round over Huff Bay, Rosie saw her young soldiers digging a ditch.

The journey back to Port Roger was smooth and uneventful and Rosie was soon looking over her script for the twelve noon broadcast extolling the virtues and rewards of the regime for the people of the Faraways.

Meticulously-kept records, which later fell into British Army hands, indicated that Corporal Gomez was shot by firing squad at a time which must have been about half an hour after the General's plane took off.

★ ★ ★

Albert hated his Marranesian helmet. It had seemed a good idea at the time and he had promised himself an item of headgear, if only to give the trilby a rest. It was looking a bit battered at the moment and so he had thrown the helmet out of the boat before he fell off the jetty into the water at Huff Bay.

The problem now was trying to get fit and be soldier-like. He had been provided with denim battle dress, top and trousers, but he found it very difficult to keep them together. The more items he put in the trouser pockets, the lower the trousers got so that the crutch came closer to the knees and a gap of vest showed above the belt as the top pulled under the arms. The problem with the helmet was that it bounced up and down brutally on his head when he ran. However did Erroll Flynn manage in those war movies?

Wentworth Stringer and Albert were exercising and rehearsing for 'a show', which Wentworth Stringer had planned for the following day. Each day at 11.30 in the morning he would broadcast to the islanders, giving them news (in so far as he could) enlarging on the exploits of Blue Fox and his merry men and reinforcing the belief in the minds of the islanders that whatever the shortcomings of the British, they were paragons of virtue compared to a Marxist dictatorship.

It was, however, one thing to broadcast the news. It was quite another thing to try and make the news. This could only be done by attacking the Marranesians and creating incidents which would become common knowledge. The problem about Huff Bay was that, like everywhere outside Port Roger, it was so remote that the rest of the islanders listening to their radios would not know for themselves whether the incidents described by Blue Fox had actually happened, or maybe he was making them up. Wentworth Stringer noted, for example, that Rosie had made no mention of the Huff Bay attack in her most recent broadcast. Wentworth Stringer felt she was doing the right thing from her standpoint. If she referred to Huff Bay she would give the incident credence and an extra news profile. She would, however, have to be careful because if Blue Fox managed to get in a spectacular success that was seen or heard in Port Roger, then that would have to be referred to in one of her broadcasts.

Wentworth Stringer had sent Rollo and Kelp away to reconnoitre the vicinity of the Port Roger airfield with a view to an attack being mounted. Rollo was a thoroughly reliable chap when it came to this type of operation. He had been a National Service infantry officer and although rather out of condition these days, he knew what he was about and as for Kelp, he was quite simply invaluable. Kelp would be recommended for a decoration after this was all over.

In the meantime, Wentworth Stringer had selected the motor transport unit at Ketchup Creek for the attention of Blue Fox. There had been a tiny garage and a petrol pump at Ketchup Creek long before the invasion. The repair facilities consisted of a low shed with a corrugated iron roof. The Marranesians had located an MT Sergeant and some mechanics at Ketchup Creek and they had done this, presumably, because the only roads on that part of the island intersected close to the corrugated hut and there was something of a junction.

The Ketchup Creek 'depot' was not a very good site from a defensive point of view, but the Marranesians had not been expecting to be attacked. The road junction and the depot buildings were overlooked by a low plateau and a wood ran quite close to one corner of the buildings. Wentworth Stringer had chosen the wood as the point of attack because it was on the same level as the buildings into which he wanted to fire. Despite the superficial attraction of firing from the plateau, he had decided to leave one of Kelp's cousins — who was useful with a rifle and excited by an AK47 — in that position while he and Albert came through the wood to the nearest buildings. The other Kelp cousin was to guard the horses in the wood and to lead them to safety after the attack — all three of them on horseback. Their retreat would be covered by the cousin on the hill.

As they were without Rollo and Kelp, the aim of this attack was to destroy vehicles if possible and not to try to overrun the buildings. Once again the element of surprise was to be paramount.

Albert had been on a horse for the first time the day before, but Wentworth Stringer reckoned it was worth the risk because they would have been far too slow getting away on foot. Albert had not particularly enjoyed the experience of being on a horse but he had clung on and discovered various muscles he did not know he had.

Apart from the horse, and trying to get fit and keep his trousers up and his helmet on, Albert's preoccupation had been the examination of the RPG7 anti-tank weapon, which they were to use at Ketchup Creek. Even Kelp had not fired one of these before, but there was general agreement as to loading and aiming and then a lot of talk about the firing position and the need to pull the weapon tightly into the shoulder to minimise recoil. The safety catch procedures were discussed at length. The one thing it was not possible to do was to fire practice rounds because there weren't any. The first practice rounds would be the real thing.

The group blacked up their faces in mid-afternoon and got into the boat with a Kelp cousin. After a twenty minute journey they were tying up the boat in a shaded mooring and meeting the other Kelp cousin, who was on horseback and led three other horses. They mounted and set off in silence for the eight mile trek. For once there was no rain and little wind and Albert and Wentworth Stringer shared briefly a sense of physical well-being garnished with a touch of moral superiority that while people in London no doubt exploded with rage, they were actually engaging the Queen's enemies.

As they entered the wood near Ketchup Creek, they halted. Wentworth Stringer had a final briefing on timings and evacuation procedures with the Cousin on the Hill, who then moved off to take up position. The three now dismounted and the Cousin in the Wood took up his position in a small clearing with all three horses. Wentworth Stringer and Albert went forward quickly on foot, Albert's bloody helmet still banging up and down.

Presently the redoubtable duo were in a ditch at the very edge of the wood no more than fifty yards from the end of the building with the corrugated tin roof. The end of the building had a small outhouse, probably the latrine, protruding from it at the point nearest to the wood. An armoured personnel carrier was parked in front of the building, giving the watchers in the wood an end-on view of it. As they took up position, they could hardly believe their good fortune because a second armoured personnel carrier was coming slowly along the road from their right and would cross right in front of them in a side-on profile.

'OK, Albert. I'll take the end-on APC on the left. It's stationary but the angle is harder. You take the APC coming along the road. You have got it side-on, so wait until it's right in front of the building and then squeeze the trigger. You can't miss. As soon as you fire, I'll fire and then the Cousin on the Hill will fire to keep their heads down as we prepare to leave.' Wentworth Stringer was precise. Albert's mouth was dry. This was it. The APC rumbled along the road.

Albert squinted through the sight in a way he thought he remembered from the Army Cadet Force at school. He pulled the weapon into his shoulder because the recoil bothered him a bit. As he squinted through the sight, Albert saw a large Marranesian with Sergeant's stripes on his arm walk to the small protruding building at the end of the corrugated iron building. The man was carrying what looked like a newspaper. He opened a door and went in. The APC rumbled closer. Albert decided to work out the aiming point by aiming at the end of the corrugated iron building and then dropping down two notches to where the APC would be in the road just below the buildings.

Albert's heart was thumping now and he was breathing quickly, which made it harder to hold the weapon sight steady. As the APC came into his frame, Albert felt himself being drawn, in that extraordinary but inexorable way of human affairs, towards the object he did not want — the hut of corrugated iron — and away from the object he did want, the APC. He squinted, found his aiming point, held his breath and squeezed the trigger.

There was a huge flash, some part of the foresight hit him in the face, and his right shoulder appeared to have been removed it hurt so much. The APC was still there, although it had now stopped and was deciding what to do. The extension to the corrugated iron building had disappeared totally. Years later some pieces of plastic lavatory seat were found embedded in a tree. The Sergeant was never seen again.

Wentworth Stringer had fired the second he heard Albert fire and his APC spurted flame and then began to burn in earnest. A hatch opened and a figure started to struggle out. The Cousin on the Hill began firing. The corrugated iron building was on fire and figures were running in all directions, attracting the attentions of the Cousin on the Hill. The unscathed APC remembered that it carried a 20 millimetre cannon and began to loose off rounds at random.

'Come on,' said Wentworth Stringer, 'before they get lucky.'

They turned and made their way back into the wood to the Cousin in the Wood and started on the journey back. After a brief pause they were joined by the Cousin on the Hill and they urged the horses to a trot to make good their escape.

'I'm sorry I missed,' said Albert when they were safely under way on the boat.

'Don't worry,' said Wentworth Stringer. 'Those things are never easy to fire the first time and you certainly spoilt the day of that Marranesian Sergeant. Just think of his letter to Kellogg's. *Dear Mr Kellogg, I have been taking your Bran Flakes. Today I found the mixture explosive.*' They laughed. Albert was glad to have Wentworth Stringer's approbation and friendship. Despite the discomfort, they had achieved something and Albert couldn't help noticing that he had remained totally dry throughout the operation. He was still thinking about this when he caught his foot on a capstan and fell off the jetty on their return.

★ ★ ★

It was time for tea at Government House. Rosie had made her noon broadcast without any mention of the Huff Bay incident. On reflection she felt the General was right militarily, but she had been hurt by his firmness at the time. Still this was a military operation and he was the Commander of the forces and not a political leader.

Tea was brought in by the General's personal orderly, Pedro.

'Thank you, Pedro,' said Rosie. 'You have heard how we English like our tea.'

'Oh yes, Ma'am. Warm the pot first.'

Rosie laughed. 'How long have you worked for the General?'

'Ten years, Ma'am. Since the time the General had just been made a Colonel.'

'Where was that?'

'In Gazebo, Ma'am. We were stationed in the Torquemada Barracks.'

Something flashed in Rosie's mind. The name of the barracks. She felt sure it had figured in an Amnesty International report. But the Army was a large organisation and the General would not have been involved with that sort of thing.

'The General still has a photograph of his fellow officers who were with him at the Torquemada Barracks. I'll find it.'

Pedro was eager to please. If Rosie was happy, then Pedro would be all right — for a while. Pedro had gone into the General's study and returned with the sort of framed group photograph of officers which can be found in sitting rooms around the world. He handed it to Rosie. The General — then a Colonel — was sitting on the front row next to the Commanding Officer. Rosie looked at the faces. They looked just like any Army officers she had ever seen and she was about to hand the photographic back when her attention was caught by one face. She looked at that face. The officer was standing directly behind her Luis. He was younger and of lower rank if he was standing.

'Who is this?' she asked.

Pedro looked at the photograph. 'Lieutenant Estepona, Ma'am.'

Rosie handed back the photograph. Of course that was the name: Lieutenant Estepona. Her Select Committee on Human Rights had heard evidence last year from people who claimed to have been tortured by Lieutenant Estepona at the Torquemada Barracks. She thanked Pedro and he left. She must not fall prey to guilt by association, she thought. Just another item for the memory bank, perhaps.

★ ★ ★

Rollo had briefed Wentworth Stringer carefully. Time spent on reconnaissance is never wasted, it has been said, and Rollo and Kelp had cased the airfield very carefully indeed. They had, in particular, taken note of the arrival and departure times of the large C130 Hercules aircraft that were so vital to the Marranesian resupply.

The airfield itself was quite well defended, with strong points at all the main vantage positions. An attack on the airfield was as unnecessary as it was out of the question. This was the Wentworth Stringer theory, which he outlined over the kitchen table at a large farmhouse about fifteen miles from the airfield and which was now Blue Fox's temporary headquarters. The group had joined up once again with Albert, dried out and in yet another pair of boots. This farmhouse was owned by Frond, the other Executive Council member, who together with Mulch had accompanied the parliamentary delegation on their visit to the outlying parts of the island. What a long time ago that now seemed to them all.

'My thinking goes like this,' began Wentworth Stringer, looking round at them all. 'The real damage that we can cause is to interfere with their resupply at the airfield. There are two ways in which this can be done. One way is to capture or destroy the airfield so that it cannot be used. That is obviously out of the question. The other way is to shoot down some aircraft about to land and suddenly they would have a crisis. They would not know when, if ever, it was going to be safe to fly in. We would not need to be successful every time if we can have some successes. We can then throw doubt in their minds. Every flight that we can delay or divert is one flight less with resupply for their war effort. That has to be good news.' He paused and looked intently round the group.

'Here is what we will do. Kelp and Rollo have been watching aircraft landing. Because there is only one runway running east to west and prevailing winds are westerlies, all flights apart from emergencies land from the east into the wind. All aircraft have to line up their approach ten miles out, usually after a preliminary circuit of the airfield. They are then controlled in the usual way onto the runway. During their approach they have to pass over the Mount Hernia range of hills. On our observation they are no more than five to eight hundred feet above ground level as they fly over the ridge. In that position they are a prime target for our Stringer missile. We do not think that we have been seen yet doing our recce work. The incredible thing to me is that they operate as though there is no war going on. They have no patrols out from the airfield and no observation posts on the high ground — at least not yet. They soon will have when we hit our first target.' Everyone laughed.

'Any questions so far?'

'Yes,' said Rollo. 'The problem for us as I see it is the considerable variation from flight to flight between the points on the ridge over which the aircraft fly. In terms of aircraft navigation they are pretty accurate to within a few hundred yards. They have flown some hundreds of miles and the runway is straight ahead of them. For us on the ground, however, it makes a heck of a difference if one aircraft is directly overhead and the next one is almost outside the performance range. What do we do?'

'Good question. We will have to have two firing units, each taking one half of the approach arc. From our positions we will have plenty of time to decide which unit will engage. The one thing we don't know is when these flights will come. From our observation, flights arrive in late morning. They seem nervous about hanging around and take off again in the afternoon. I am sure the enemy would like a flight every day, but at the moment the frequency is about one every other day. After lunch Frond has said we can use his big barn to practise drills on the weapon, which is jolly kind of him. At first light the firing parties will recce the ground and select their firing positions.'

The practice drills took place and then the four slipped out in the dusk to examine the ridge. The aim was to return before first light and get themselves dug in and still before they could be seen by anyone using binoculars along the ridge. Radio silence was to be maintained, a system of small flags having been devised. Wentworth Stringer would allocate the firing unit to fire using a red flag for himself, blue for Rollo and green for both units to fire. Rollo would train his binos on Wentworth Stringer and act on his flag.

The group returned before first light, tracking carefully over the ridge to the two positions they had earmarked. They worked hard with the entrenching tools and got themselves well down by first light. Rollo and Kelp had opened their coffee thermos by 0F 30 to keep them warm as they talked about Kelp's hopes for the Islands after the war.

Wentworth Stringer and Albert talked about Rosie Long and what a strange world politics was. The morning dragged on and by midday with no aircraft, the Frond sandwiches were finished. No aircraft came over all day. Shortly before dusk Wentworth Stringer used his yellow flag, which meant *withdraw*, and they headed back to their operational base camp which was in a barn about four miles from the ridge. The Frond farm was a further ten miles away. They were very tired and extremely disappointed, but Wentworth Stringer kept spirits up and pointed out they were odds on favourites to have a target tomorrow. The best thing they could do was get some sleep, which they all did.

The following day the exercise was repeated, this time without the hard work with the entrenching tools. Once more they settled in to wait and once again there was no sign of any aircraft. Wentworth Stringer looked at his watch. It was nearly noon. Then he heard it, the clear and unmistakable rumble of an aircraft approaching. He raised his binoculars to try and get a fix on his direction. It was harder than he thought it would be to work out the line of approach. When he was sure, he showed the small blue flag to Rollo.

Rollo put down the glasses and turned to Kelp. 'It's ours. Over to you, hot shot.'

Kelp and Rollo had worked on the Stinger manual in Spanish and made what sense they could of it. Kelp was now fixing the C130 in the cross hairs of the aiming sight. The aircraft came closer and closer, lower and lower to the ridge, louder and louder in engine noise. The aircraft was so low now that they felt they could reach up and touch it. Rollo tapped Kelp twice on the shoulder and he fired.

For a moment nothing seemed to happen as the aircraft passed overhead and then a flicker of flame spouted from the port engine. Still the aircraft flew on but the flames were now spreading and one of the starboard engines was also ablaze. The stricken aircraft bucked violently from side to side and began to descend. It was now about half a mile from the end of the runway and about two hundred yards further on it hit the ground with a colossal explosion, which shook every building in Port Roger, and then there was a tremendous fire.

The four stared awestruck at their handiwork before Wentworth Stringer gave the yellow flag and they withdrew. This time they force marched all fifteen miles back to the Frond farm.

Rosie Long was concluding the twelve noon broadcast and was not, or tried not to be, disconcerted by the explosion. The news that was given to her and which she faithfully reproduced in her next bulletin was that the C130 had crashed on approach to the airfield. No mention would be made of the fact that the aircraft had been shot down, but Wentworth Stringer would repair that omission in his own broadcast the next morning.

While the islanders were weighing up the next day the conflicting reasons as to why the aircraft had crashed, there was one piece of news which they had gleaned from the World Service and there was no arguing about this. The British Task Force to retake the Faraway Islands had set sail from British waters that morning.

9

The War Cabinet

♦

LORD MAFEKING NOTED that the Prime Minister never seemed to walk on these occasions; rather, she bustled, with all the movement appearing to be below the knee, a style perfected on a thousand factory floor and market square walkabouts, although they were spared the handshakes.

The Prime Minister swept into the Cabinet Room and took her place halfway down the table facing out towards Horse Guards Parade. On her immediate right sat the Secretary to the Cabinet, Sir Philip Prolix, and on his right were three more Private Secretaries, who had entered the room from the double doors at the end which led to the Cabinet Office Secretariat.

Above and behind the Prime Minister hung the portrait of Sir Robert Walpole, the first holder of the Office that is now known as Prime Minister and First Lord of the Treasury. In happier times when defence was not on the agenda, Mafeking allowed his attention to stray to Walpole's face. The eyes, although not unfriendly, were somewhat cynical.

'Never mind the collapse of the secondary banks and the losses on Johnson Matthey, you should have been here for the South Sea Bubble, now that really was something,' he could have been saying.

Mafeking was once again aware of a prickly sensation on the backs of his hands, a sensation which gradually spread up his arms, and it took all of his strength of mind not to scratch vigorously. Every time he came to a Cabinet meeting and had to take a part of any prominence he experienced these same symptoms, which resembled heat rash. He knew it was nerves and he knew his nerves were caused by the Prime Minister.

The Prime Minister began the meeting. 'Secretary of State

for Defence, will you give us a review of the military situation, please.'

Mafeking felt an increase in the prickliness on the backs of his hands as he studied the folder on the table in front of him.

'Prime Minister, if you agree, we should ask CDS to give us his latest report and military appreciation.'

'Very well. Chief of the Defence Staff.'

The Prime Minister preferred to avoid using the acronyms by which everyone from the doorman up was known at the Ministry of Defence. Admiral Halliard cleared his throat. Mafeking usually found that in Cabinet meetings whenever it was not his turn to speak the prickliness on his hands eased, but in this case the prickliness seemed, if anything, to intensify because it was his man, CDS, who was about to hold forth. Although the Prime Minister had met the CDS before, she had not been subjected to one of his presentations, as it had been his predecessor who had briefed her when she first came into office on the scale of the Soviet threat, the grasp of UK military intelligence and the state of UK nuclear readiness. Mafeking had been justifiably concerned that one of the Admiral's staccato presentations might have the War Cabinet somewhat mystified. The loathsome Brian and Jolyon had been given the task of rehearsing the Admiral with a speech that would include at least an occasional verb. In addition, his ship models had been impounded.

'Prime Minister,' the Admiral began, 'the Faraway Islands situation not good. Islands occupied by Marranesian forces. Our forces prisoner. Marranesians reinforcing Islands by air. We have assembled Task Force. Will sail tomorrow. Time needed to get close to Faraway Islands approximately 50 days. Nuclear submarine HMS *Relapse* already despatched from Gibraltar. Time to get to war zone 28 days. Task Force includes aircraft carriers *Indubitable* and *Ineluctable*. County class type 42 *Rutland*, *Middlesex* and *East Yorkshire* and 4 Type 21 frigates from the Anal class *Ordure*, *Orifice*, *Obloquy* and *Obstreperous*, plus the support vessels *Rectum* and *Up Yours*, and the converted civil vessel *Pacific Purveyor*. In all, we have 37 ships taken up from trade. Morale good.'

'Did I understand the Chief of the Defence Staff to say that HMS *Relapse* has already been despatched? May we know by whose authority, Prime Minister?' It was Woodcock, as quick as a flash, with the top item on his Foreign Office briefing paper.

'By my authority, Prime Minister,' interjected Mafeking.

'As HMS *Relapse* was already at Gibraltar, it seemed wise to start her underway so as not to lose any time and also to be seen to be doing something.'

'Prime Minister, I must support the Defence Secretary on that point. The party in the country is looking for action,' said Brilliant.

'I assume that fresh orders can be given to *Relapse*.' The Prime Minister was half questioning, half asserting.

'Oh yes, Prime Minister,' said the Admiral. 'Ship to surface. Messages passed.'

The Prime Minister stared carefully at the Admiral. The Admiral had never fired a shot in anger. Now he wished he had had that experience, if only to compare it with this firing line.

The Prime Minister spoke. 'HMS *Relapse* must continue her present course.'

'Thank you, Prime Minister,' said the Admiral gratefully, glancing for approval at Mafeking, who did not return the glance.

'Foreign Secretary. Your report, please.'

'Prime Minister, I am going to Brussels in the morning to meet European Community Foreign Ministers. I intend to get their support, perhaps in the form of a joint statement or at least an agreement to support us in the United Nations. We have requested a meeting of the Security Council and I will shortly be meeting with the UN Secretary-General.'

'That terrible little man,' the Prime Minister hissed.

'Indeed, Prime Minister, but he is all that there is ...'

'He once had the impertinence to tell me that women had no place in politics.' She half-turned to Johnnie Mollusc as she said this. He smiled indulgently. Woodcock was still in mid-sentence.

'The United Nations ...' he began again.

'That wretched little man would never have been Secretary-General if the Americans hadn't been so weak and feeble.' She spat out these words. 'They were obsessed with currying favour with Latin America.'

Everyone nodded sympathetically with this trial *in absentia* of the unfortunate UN Secretary General. At least they were not in the dock themselves, although some of them felt a twinge of sympathy for the man should he ever meet the PM again. Woodcock was still high and dry, attempting to complete his report as the Prime Minister fizzed and crackled, apparently only using his phrases as a springboard for further tirades.

'Now let me see.' The Prime Minister had decided that although the meeting had virtually just begun, she would sum up. This was partly an attempt to impose her predilections and presuppositions on her colleagues, but more usually an attempt to force them to justify their positions and argue against her if they dared. It was a standard technique which she invariably employed.

'Our Task Force is assembling for despatch tomorrow and we are seen to be acting firmly. We will gain support from our friends around the world and from the Americans. They will support us.' Mafeking noticed that as the Prime Minister concluded this remark her tongue flicked out and back very rapidly like a lizard. He had seen her do this before and usually it accompanied some very positive assertion that she was making.

'We still have work to do on the Americans, Prime Minister,' said Woodcock, with all the confidence of the newly-appointed. 'As you said, they are anxious about their position in Latin America.'

'We are anxious about our position on the Faraway Islands,' boomed the Prime Minister.

'Of course we are, Prime Minister. I just think it would be unwise to underestimate the difficulties the Americans are still in over this matter. It is not simple for them,' said Woodcock quietly.

'We think it is perfectly simple for the Americans. Simple enough for even them to grasp it,' snorted the Prime Minister. 'We require their support in diplomatic terms, in communications satellites and in staging and refuelling at Whitsun Island. That is what we require, in return for the support we have given them (a) when they invaded a Commonwealth Caribbean island without telling us first, (b) when they sank a clearly marked hospital ship loaded with nursing sisters many miles from the Gulf war zone, (c) when they shot a Cuban diplomat who was about to defect to the west in mistake for a diplomat whom we wanted to accidentally escape anyway, and (d) when we allowed them to use airbases in this country to bomb a country in North Africa which had dared to fire on one of their planes. That is why we are owed some support.'

'Will the President ...' began Woodcock courageously in the face of the hurricane.

'The dear President,' the Prime Minister suddenly cooed. Certainly things American seemed to be different when the dear old President came into the conversation.

'Items (b) and (c) to which I referred a moment ago would have been operational matters outside the President's span of control.' The listening colleagues thought the Prime Minister was going to say *comprehension*, but she actually said, almost benignly, *control*, as one might about the family dog. Good boy Rover. A dog would never be elected to high office in the United States, thought Mafeking. They're not nearly sentimental enough about dogs in America. Now over here a dog — or a bitch — could be elected Prime Minister. Mafeking glanced up quickly with prickly heat mounting. The gaze was on him. Had he missed a question? Was there something on the blackboard that he could not decipher.

'Secretary of State for Defence. Do you find co-operation with the Americans easy to achieve?' came the question.

'Oh yes, Prime Minister. We have close operational ties with the Americans, as CDS will explain,' replied Mafeking.

The Chief of Defence Staff cleared his throat. 'Americans good chaps. On the whole.'

'You were saying about the President, Prime Minister,' Mafeking prompted rather neatly and off she went again.

'The dear President did remember to call me as their planes were taking off for their Caribbean adventure so we should be thankful for small mercies. I am sure that I can persuade him to support us if I can make sure to telephone during his quite short waking hours. In the meantime we have the disgusting American Secretary of State coming to Chequers for the weekend. I am going to ask Derek' (here she referred to her much lampooned husband) 'to come up with some vulgar stories for me to use.'

'We will certainly do all we can to bring the Americans along with us, Prime Minister,' said Woodcock.

'We will succeed,' said the Prime Minister grimly.

'I wondered, Prime Minister, if we could have a word or two about our longer term strategy, longer term than this weekend, that is.' Woodcock was persistent and was using his position skilfully because the Prime Minister clearly liked him.

'Please continue, Foreign Secretary,' invited the Prime Minister as she examined a note put in front of her by one of her officials. Woodcock had the floor and all eyes were on him.

'At this time we can have but one aim and that is to put an end as soon as possible to Marranesian occupation of British sovereign territory, the Faraway Islands. It seems that there are two ways in which we can achieve this aim. One way is for the Task Force to sail on, make a successful landing and force the surrender of Marranesian forces. The other way is to use the time that the Task Force takes to sail to the Faraway Islands to exert maximum diplomatic pressure — in fact to mount a massive diplomatic offensive to force the Marranesians to withdraw. The Marranesians clearly now realise that they have gone too far. They have miscalculated. They have misread our intentions. They are looking for an escape route, a way to get off the hook,' concluded Woodcock.

'Oh, are they, indeed?' The Prime Minister's voice was as hard as granite.

'They certainly have miscalculated and they will be made to pay dearly for their miscalculation. Looking back on it now, I don't think one can entirely blame the Marranesians for misreading our intentions. Firstly, we had talks with their representatives in New York and discussed informally ways of setting up some form of joint authority over the Islands. Secondly, when the talks got nowhere, the Ministry of Defence decided to withdraw HMS *Reluctance*, thus giving further encouragement to the hawks in Marranesia.'

'The Foreign Office line has been consistent throughout. Look for ways of handing over the Faraways. That message is very clear,' the Prime Minister flashed angrily. 'Then the Ministry of Defence joined in the rush to appease.' This was accompanied by a scowl at Lord Mafeking. 'What the Foreign Office seem to be saying now is that we should continue the discredited policy of the past few months. The country will not wear this. The country wants us to throw out the Marranesians.' A further Prime Ministerial assertion with characteristic set of mouth and jaw.

'I agree with that, Prime Minister. All I am saying is that we should use the time that it takes for the Task Force to get there to isolate the Marranesians. We will still need friends in the EC and the United Nations. However infuriating it may be to us ...'

'It most certainly is,' interrupted the Prime Minister.

'As the completely innocent party, there will be those who will urge us to avoid using force and go for a negotiated settlement,' continued Woodcock.

'Pah!' The Prime Minister flung up her hands. 'Our territory is invaded so we are to seek a negotiated settlement! I never heard such balderdash in my life!'

'Prime Minister.' It was Lord Mollusc. 'We are all agreed on the objective and I'm sure we accept the Foreign Secretary's advice that despite being completely and utterly the wronged and injured party, we will still need friends for when the shooting starts. It cannot be wrong, I would have thought, to intensify our diplomatic campaign in the time we still have at our disposal. The real bottom line issue is, having intensified our diplomatic campaign — we hope successfully — and the fleet having arrived off the Faraways, what do we do if the Marranesians still refuse to back down? They have made one miscalculation. They may think that even having gone all that way we would not want to risk invading the Islands. There will come a time when all the diplomatic talk has to stop and for us it will be action or back down. Seems common sense to me.'

Good old Johnnie Mollusc! A common sense analysis and a shrewd dart at the jumped-up johnny in charge of the Foreign Office.

'Defence Secretary.' It was prickly heat time again. 'What would you do at that time?' The question was slow and deliberate.

'I would invade the Islands and I know that CDS believes we can do it.'

'Absolutely. Absolutely. Chaps first class. First class,' said the Admiral, stroking the braid on his sleeve for comfort.

'Chancellor of the Duchy.' The Prime Minister invited the Chairman of the Party to speak, using the title of his Cabinet post.

'Given the situation that the Lord President has described, the party would expect nothing less than a successful invasion.'

'Lord Privy Seal.' The Prime Minister now invited Tommy Tunstall as Leader of the House to make a contribution.

'I agree totally with the Chancellor of the Duchy. If the Marranesians haven't backed down by the time the Task Force is in position we will have to invade.'

'Chief Whip.'

William Hopper attempted to focus his eyes on the Prime Minister and stop them constantly roaming the table. 'The party in the House will want the invasion, although they would prefer casualties not to be in marginal seats.'

'I am sure the Commander in Chief will arrange for the main assault to be made by units drawn exclusively from strong Tory seats.' Woodcock was indulging his own brand of sarcasm. He was irritated by Mollusc's manoeuvring and the way in which the others were ranging with the Defence Secretary. He would have to beware, however, because sarcasm, or indeed any form of wit, was not appreciated at the Cabinet table.

'Foreign Secretary.' The request was almost *sotto voce.*

'I have no problem with anything that our colleagues have said. If the situation should be as the Lord President described it then we must carry our policy through and if that means we must invade the Islands, so be it.'

There was quiet approval for the Foreign Secretary's first performance. He had been gutsy without being foolhardy and shown neat footwork to avoid painting himself into a corner. Woodcock seemed able to say even commonplace things in a tone which was interesting and even flattering to her. It was possible that the Prime Minister even found Woodcock attractive, although this line of thinking took Mafeking into the realms of the unfathomable, leading as it did to assessments of her sexuality. In repose she was a handsome woman, although her neck seemed fatter and more lined than he remembered.

The Prime Minister now indicated that it was time to get on with the war and the first meeting of Cabinet Committee OD (SP) came to an end.

As the others gathered their papers and made to leave the Cabinet room the Prime Minister indicated to Woodcock that she would like him to stay. He came and stood at the end of the table as she got up from her chair and joined him at the end of the table. The Chief Whip, as the last to leave, closed the door behind him.

'Roger, we need your enthusiasm but we also need a victory. Nothing less will do. I'm sure you understand,' and she patted him affectionately on the forearm.

'Quite so, Prime Minister.'

While the Prime Minister and Woodcock were having their brief *tête-à-tête*, the others were walking down the corridor to the front door of Number Ten. It was clear to Mafeking that much though the Prime Minister disliked him, he and his Ministry represented the means and hope of glory, whereas Woodcock — liked by the Prime Minister — rode the unpromising nag, by appeasement out of compromise.

Mafeking and Johnnie Mollusc were to have lunch at the House of Lords, so they rode in Mafeking's Granada, driven by Sergeant Banger, who would shortly be compiling his reports and assessments of the meeting just ended.

Johnnie Mollusc was quick with his back seat analysis of the situation. 'Roger Woodcock is making a big play for a diplomatic solution which sees the Marranesians off the Islands and no British losses. It would be a terrific coup for him if he can do it. Rather like winning the VC in your first battle.'

Roger Woodcock was thinking the very same thoughts as he walked along the most important corridor in Britain.

10

Chequers

◆

LORD MAFEKING HAD BECOME so totally dependent on his support staff that he was no longer confident of his ability to cross the road on his own and even if he did make it over, it would probably turn out to be the wrong road. When it came to car journeys, he simply settled himself in the back seat of the black Ministry of Defence Granada and Sergeant Banger did the rest.

The destination today was Chequers. As it was a Sunday there was a lot of traffic heading westward out of London to make the most of the spring sunshine. As roadworks were in progress on the Westway flyover, Sergeant Banger turned off and used his knowledge of the back doubles around Shepherds Bush to catch up any lost time.

The plan was to meet at Chequers at eleven o'clock and have a brief discussion with all the War Cabinet members before the American Secretary of State arrived at eleven thirty. He was flying into Heathrow in a US Air Force aircraft and would be brought to Chequers by helicopter.

Mafeking was using the time to glance at his notes relating to the assembling of the fleet. His Ministry of Defence people really were excelling themselves in the complicated work necessary to identify and locate and, in effect, commandeer civilian ships that would be an essential part of the Task Force. Most, if not all, of these vessels would require some modifications to be made to them, either to turn them into troop ships or, in the case of container ships, to make them suitable to house and support Harrier aircraft and helicopters.

By now Sergeant Banger was negotiating the main street of Great Missenden and they would soon be at Chequers. He read more about co-operation between his Ministry and industry. Work was being carried out overnight and over the weekend at breakneck speed. Procurement red tape that usually required months of preliminary studies had been swept away. The job was being done. The arsenals of England were hard at work. Henry V would have been proud of them. Maybe we needed a crisis every Friday, mused Mafeking as the car turned into the tree-lined drive at Chequers and stopped for identification at the police post.

Once the constable had ticked Mafeking's name on the list and cross-checked the car number, it was all right to proceed along a straight narrow road which interesected with the original drive at ninety degrees. Then the car had to turn right and almost at once left into the entrance courtyard. The original drive, which ran from a bend in the main road, led straight to the Elizabethan manor house given to the nation by Viscount Lee in 1917 for the exclusive use of the Prime Minister of the day. The entrance courtyard was quite small, gravelled, with a circular piece of lawn in the middle. Official cars would drop their passengers at the door and then go round the outside of the house to the rear kitchen entrance. Sergeant Banger always liked visiting Chequers because he always ate well. The catering was very efficiently run by a Women's Royal Air Force Wing Commander and organised and staffed on a tri-service basis.

Sergeant Banger drove off towards food and Lord Mafeking was admitted by a leading Wren. He made his way from the front door to the entrance hall, where an RAF Corporal indicated that the meeting would be in the Great Parlour on the first floor. As Mafeking went up the stairs he heard Johnnie Mollusc's voice. He was talking to Woodcock.

Mafeking entered the dark oak-panelled room and greeted everyone. He was not the last to arrive and he heard Tommy Tunstall bustling up the stairs behind him. Coffee was being served by orderlies from a side table and Mafeking obtained a black coffee. If he had dared to, he would have fortified his coffee with something stronger because it was going to be that kind of meeting.

William Hopper was endlessly scanning the room as usual, his eyes seeking to catch an errant non-Conservative fly that might have strayed onto the window pane. The Chief of the Defence staff was in civilian dress so as not to upstage the American

Secretary of State who, although a four star Admiral, had retired from the service and was now therefore a civilian.

The Chairman of the party, hair stylishly tossed, was talking with a coffee cup in his hand to Johnnie Mollusc and Roger Woodcock as the Prime Minister swept into the room. Everyone at once took their places at the table.

'We're seeing this horrible man. I'm sorry, but I will not even try and pretend that I like him. To think I have to watch him eat as well. What do we want to achieve? Foreign Secretary?'

'This is our first meeting with Admiral Legover since the Faraways crisis began. We need American support diplomatically and, of course, logistically in terms of the use of Whitsun Island. He wants to probe our intentions, to find out if we're really serious.'

'What ?!' shrieked the Prime Minister.

'Prime Minister, I am advised by telegram from our post in Washington that the Americans do want to satisfy themselves as to our intentions,' said the Foreign Secretary quietly but firmly.

'Then we will indeed be able to satisfy them,' said the Prime Minister in a particularly authoritative tone. 'How are the fleet preparations going, Defence Secretary?'

'Very well indeed, Prime Minister. I'll give you a detailed report by mid afternoon today.'

No time for prickly heat this time; it was straight in and get on with it. Mafeking felt relieved. Relieved that the operational arrangements were coming together with commendable speed. Relieved that the Prime Minister did not want to interfere in operational matters.

The unmistakable sound of a helicopter overhead caused the meeting to end. They all stood up and trooped downstairs and made their way to the side of the old house looking towards the lawn on which the helicopter would soon land. The helicopter was an RAF Puma and it circled the landing site twice, well aware that the landing would be a Royal Command performance and keen to avoid the many trees in the park.

The Prime Minister remained back at the door opening onto the lawns; not for her any ruffling of coiffure because of down draught. The RAF crew suddenly decided to land on the rear lawn rather than the front lawn, causing the greeting party to rush from one side of Chequers to the other and then back again when the original front lawn was selected. It was Roger Woodcock who went forward to do the greeting because he was to welcome his opposite number, the Secretary of State, Admiral Warren B Legover.

The helicopter landed and a crewman leaped out smartly and put down the steps and suddenly there he was, hero of the Korean War, former Supreme Allied Commander in Europe, stocky, aggressive, bad tempered. A man of few words, all of them profane. Why on earth one of the highest offices of state, short only of the Presidency itself, should have gone to this man, few people on either side of the Atlantic could begin to guess. In some quarters it was suggested that he was one of those relatively few people with whom the President felt comfortable. Anyway, here he was, the representative of the most powerful nation in the West.

Mafeking noted with irritation that Legover was saluting the helicopter crew, although as a civilian he had no uniform and no ability to give such salutes. Woodcock stepped forward and greeted the Admiral with a friendly handshake. They walked together towards the house as the helicopter engines were turned off and the blades ceased to twirl.

'Hello, Prime Minister. How are you today?' came the bluff greeting.

'How was your journey, Admiral?' asked the Prime Minister, and then wished she hadn't.

'Oh, we tore along in the chopper. Just like shit off a shovel.'

'Shall we go upstairs?' said the Prime Minister stiffly, and before doing so introduced him to the members of the War Cabinet.

They all turned up the flight of stairs from the entrance hall to the Great Parlour and resumed their seats, this time making room for Admiral Legover and his Marine cohort, Colonel West. The Prime Minister began the meeting.

'We are very grateful to you for coming to see us, Admiral Legover. It is essential that each of us understands the other's position.'

'Prime Minister. The President has asked me to say that the welcomes this opportunity for me to have interfacial involvement with the possibility of encapsulating the parameters of your position,' the Admiral began.

'What, might I ask, is meant by *interfacial involvement?* It sounds faintly disgusting.'

'We're having a meeting. That's all. It's good news. But what are your plans? We're hoping to step up the diplomatic offensive and persuade them to get off the Islands. What is your action plan?'

'It is exactly that. An action plan. We're going to invade the Islands and take them back,' said the Prime Minister.

'Holy shit, Jenny! Are you serious? Do you have any idea of the risks? Oh, God!'

The Admiral was rather excited. Mafeking thought he was verging on the tired-and-emotional, but had no evidence to back that suspicion. The Prime Minister was never addressed as Jenny by anyone except the Sun newspaper, but this little creep had completely lost his cool. Mafeking reckoned that a seat at this table for this discussion had to be worth a guinea a second. He awaited the next salvo in the exchange of artillery. He did not have long to wait. Mafeking was sitting next to the Prime Minister on her left, with his prickly heat hands carefully on his lap. Roger Woodcock, as the other principal UK player, sat on the Prime Minister's right. All three had a perfect three-dimensional view of the Korean War hero, his face crumpling and distorting with a mixture of rage, disbelief and frustration.

'You are going to tell us why we won't succeed.' The Prime Minister's voice was stiff with tension.

'This operation needs more than the Dunkirk spirit,' snapped Legover, attempting to regain his composure.

'Perhaps I could remind you, Admiral Legover, that Dunkirk was a strategic withdrawal.' Otherwise known as a retreat, commented Mafeking silently. 'Perhaps we could think of D-Day if we are going back into history. Then we did it together. This time we're going on our own.'

'D-Day was across fifty or so miles of English Channel with complete air superiority. This operation that you're proposing is at the very limits of do-ability. We think that this is a no-no, a complete lemon, and what's more you'll end up with your tits jammed in the mangle.'

There are occasions in human affairs when time seems to stand still, when there is at the very epicentre of a typhoon a pool of calm and silence. Mafeking was aware of something akin to a magnetic field operating. Thinking back on it afterwards, he could have sworn he saw a starling in flight near the windows drop like a stone into the bushes, and was it a coincidence that the clock on Great Missenden Parish Church had failed to complete the striking of twelve noon?

Directly opposite they were witnessing the implosion of a human being. The dynamite in his pocket had exploded. For Admiral Legover this was a worse situation, far worse, than anything the Red Chinese threw at him in the Pusan salient. The blue laser eyes stared and stared and stared.

Try as he might, he could not meet that gaze. To Mafeking there was no doubt that Legover had easily supplanted the Secretary-General of the United Nations as the foreigner most likely to be turned to stone. At this rate he would have a special gazebo all to himself somewhere in the grounds and the helicopter would return without him, with the message *Missing in Action*.

It would have been how the Admiral would like to have gone, but to be fair to him he was, in his own phrase, in the dark stuff up to his neck and he had to summon up some reserves of order and discipline.

'Perhaps, Prime Minister,' he croaked, 'I could ask Colonel West to give the military appraisal from our perspective.'

There was a nod from across the table. Colonel West, crewcutted, dark suited, every inch the Marine Colonel, began.

'Any military operation conducted to retake the Faraway Islands by force of arms would take place at the limit — or, in our view, beyond the limit — of operational effectiveness. The Islands are around 8,000 miles from the UK and about 400 miles from the Marranesian coast and the nearest Marranesian airbases. As ever, a military conflict would turn on control of the air. As we understand it, the UK Task Force would have embarked air assets of Sea Harriers, most probably augmented by RAF Harriers which will have to be marinised and then flown to join the Task Force at Whitsun Island. There must be some doubts as to the full effectiveness in a conflict situation of RAF Harrier aircraft and crews operating for the first time from carriers.'

'The Sea Harrier itself does not yet have the new Blue Vixen radar and is therefore fair weather limited in what, one has to say, is generally agreed to be one of the worst weather situations anywhere in the world. The Marranesian Air Force has the considerable advantage of operating from its land bases with Mirage and F5 aircraft. The Marranesian Air Force is well led, well trained and at a high state of combat readiness.'

'Our information on the precise numbers of the Marranesian garrison on the Faraway Islands has not been updated as of this morning, but we already know from intelligence sources that, as of yesterday, their numbers were at least 1,500 in excess of the number we forecast can be accommodated on board the British Task Force. We understand further that the Marranesians plan to fly further reinforcements to the Islands on a regular basis. Our best estimates are that the optimum rate of reinforcement and ability of the Marranesians to absorb and deploy these reinforcements points towards a further 1,000 troops every four days.'

'This does not imply that the Marranesians can or will continue this process indefinitely. They will have a ceiling in mind, and that figure could well be in the 13-15,000 bracket. Even if this is the limit of their reinforcements, that gives the Marranesians a fifty per cent numerical advantage over the envisaged Task Force numbers. The Marranesian army is a conscript army, but its officers are mainly regulars and contain many who are fanatically loyal to the present rÈgime. We also know that a Battalion of their Paratroops are already on the island and they have a high combat rating from our military observers.'

'The fact remains that, quality considerations aside, the balance favours the defenders in contradiction to the most widely agreed and proved dictum of modern warfare, namely that the attacking force to succeed must outnumber the defenders three to one, all other things being equal.'

'None of what I have said is to imply any criticism of the superb professional forces about to be committed by Britain. I would go as far as to say that were we speaking about any other attacking force in the world, we would already have ruled out any possibility of an invasion. That cannot remove the obligation on us to be as objective as we possibly can be and to reach the conclusion that it is our belief that the proposed project is unworkable to the point of being foolhardy.'

Full marks to you, Colonel, said Mafeking silently and he wondered how many of his colleagues at the table felt the same way. Woodcock certainly would, and Mollusc probably too. Tunstall and Hopper would be utterly concerned with the politics. If the invasion succeeded, She would reign forever. If it failed, She was out.

'Tell us something, Colonel.' The Prime Minister's tone was almost conversational. Mafeking knew to be particularly on guard because the tone could again become cyclonic in the twinkling of an eyelid.

'You spoke about an obligation on *us* to be as objective as *we* can and that it is *our* belief. I noted your words. Who actually is *us* and *we* and *our*?'

'The United States, your principal ally and friend.'

'Whose subjects are at present under the jackboot of a fascist invader?'

'British subjects, Ma'am.' The Colonel was sitting up to attention.

'Do you believe that the United States would be having this debate if American subjects had been treated in this way?' the Prime Minister snarled.

Admiral Legover made no attempt to give his subordinate covering fire. He was himself clearly holed below the waterline by the whole experience and was wondering if he would make it back to port. The Colonel had done well. He had been carefully professional, everyone agreed. He then made a quip too far.

'I was only attempting to point up the imbalance in numbers and to suggest that this cannot be overcome by qualitative factors alone. This will not be the Zulu War.'

Steady, Colonel, thought Mafeking. She has a hotline to your Commander in Chief. You could be a Captain before the day is out.

'I will attribute that remark to the impetuosity of youth, Colonel West,' replied the Prime Minister, ignoring the Colonel's rows of Vietnam metals. 'Chief of Defence Staff. Perhaps you could give your comments on the reasons why we cannot succeed.'

CDS cleared his throat. 'Faraway Islands well named. Damned

long way. Like 'em to be nearer. Our chaps first class. Their chaps second and third class. Ours all volunteers. Know their tasks. Well trained. Totally committed. Theirs not totally committed. Bad weather hampers their air operations as well as ours. Same for both sides. We'll win.'

'Well, that's that, then,' said the Prime Minister with an air of triumph.

'Can I take it, Prime Minister,' interjected Woodcock, 'that we have no objection to Admiral Legover following a form of shuttle diplomacy? However remote the prospect, if the Marranesians could be persuaded to withdraw while the Task Force is sailing towards them, that would suit our purpose. Always assuming, of course, that Admiral Legover is absolutely clear that the Task Force will sail.' This was Woodcock doing his bit for the Foreign Office and it was neatly played.

'Of course we are grateful for any diplomatic efforts that Admiral Legover cares to make, as long as our position is clear.'

'It certainly is,' whispered Legover.

The Prime Minister thought to herself that with Legover in charge of diplomatic efforts, there was no chance at all that the Marranesians would pull out. In fact with him in his present position, it was probably a miracle that there had not been a Third World War in the past few months.

'Perhaps we could just glance at the newspapers before we go to lunch. How cautious so many of them are.

Task Force being prepared, says the Observer. *Britain will fight,* the Sunday Times. This is the one I liked best from yesterday's Sun: *Stuff the Marras.* Who speaks for England now?' the Prime Minister asked rhetorically, and stood up to adjourn for lunch.

If the PM had been Golda Meir, late PM of Israel, she might have eased the tension by making a crack about her keeping parts of her anatomy out of certain old domestic appliances. But she was not, so she did not. Any one of her colleagues with the requisite combination of wit, confidence and stature could have asked the Admiral and the Colonel if they wanted to stop off for a holy shit on the way to lunch, but not one of them fitted that description, so no-one said anything. As the two Americans said to each other on the flight home, they had never seen a leader so totally dominate her subordinates.

11

The True Path

♦

ROSIE LONG REALISED that she was seriously in love with Luis Hernando because her feelings for him were totally unlike anything she had experienced for any man, her late husband included. In his case she had been carried along by shared political ideals, pints of bitter at the Durham Miners' Gala, some groping in the back of the Tribune office, and a certainty that, as a socialist item, they would help to bring about their revolution in the fortunes of working people.

Good and sound and wholesome as that relationship had been, there had been nothing of this, to Rosie, almost shockingly shameful, all-consuming lust. She longed to see Luis and to touch him. She wanted him to kiss her and make love to her. She longed to feel the hair on his back and to see his sallow face, with the dark eyes, black hair and thin moustache, bending over her.

It was said that power was a great aphrodisiac for women, but in Rosie's case it must have been the aura of strict authority which she found secretly thrilling. His Marxism made her enthusiastic, but the disquieting thoughts of the Torquemada Barracks caused her unease. Perhaps she should double her subscription to the Socialist Worker and cancel her subscription to Amnesty International.

It would soon be tea-time and the General seemed to like to return to Government House for tea. Rosie decided that this would be an extra special tea-time. She went into the bedroom and removed her clothes. She put on her negligÈe and sat down in the sitting room to await events. Presently she heard the General's footsteps and some shouted comments. He entered the room and having seen her he stopped. He turned and put his head into the corridor and arranged for the tea to be put into the conservatory.

'Something tells me that tea in here would not be a good idea.' He crossed the room and kissed her. He was carrying what looked like a flag under his arm. 'I've brought you something to remind you of home.' He unrolled a Union flag. 'To think that this will never fly in these Islands again.'

'Put it on.' The General proffered a hand and pulled Rosie out of her chair. He slipped off her negligée and wrapped the flag round her shoulders. He then stood back to admire the effect.

'Wonderful,' he said and took her in his arms. 'My northern trollop.'

'Dago,' Rosie flashed back defiantly. The blow across her face took Rosie completely by surprised.

'Trollop,' the General said again, louder this time.

'Dago,' came the immediate, but seemingly semi-conscious response.

In a flash the General had turned her round and then pulled her over his knee as he sat in the armchair. Rosie's bottom was now belaboured by her Latin lover, each blow accompanied by the word *trollop*. For Rosie this was painful, humiliating, and exquisitely pleasurable. Rosie was aware of the General spreading out the flag on the carpet before he unbuttoned his tunic and they made love.

It was some time before either of them spoke.

'Do you know that there are eight coronation mugs in this house?' asked the General.

Rosie smiled.

'And I've pissed in every one of them,' said the General with great satisfaction.

If Rosie had wanted to be particularly analytical she could have wondered if the General took a special delight in defiling all things British, but she was not so inclined. As far as she was concerned, her General Luis could piss on anyone or anything from any height he liked. She did, however, have one thing she wanted to ask him. The General had gone through to the bathroom.

'Luis,' Rosie said, raising herself on her elbow and putting a cushion behind her head. 'Were you ever at the Torquemada

Barracks in Gazebo?'

There was a sound of bathroom taps being run and then the basin being emptied. Suddenly the General, in a dark blue silk dressing gown stood in the bathroom doorway staring at her intently. 'Why do you ask?'

'I just wondered. The Barracks are quite well known — internationally, I mean.' Rosie stood up and put on her negligée as she spoke.

'Oh yes, the Barracks are known internationally all right,' snarled the General. 'By Amnesty International. Yes, I was at the Torquemada Barracks. What of it?'

'Did you know Lieutenant Estepona?'

'Of course I did. He was another officer. Why do you ask? — No, wait a minute, I think I know. He was the officer accused by the London-based Amnesty International of being in charge of torture in the Torquemada Barracks and I suppose you and your other British do-gooding socialist friends want to make a big things of this. Is that right?'

'My Select Committee investigated human rights abuses or, rather, allegations of such abuses, concerning the Torquemada Barracks. I seem to remember there were seventeen allegations.' Rosie thought the General was going to explode. His eyes rolled and beads of perspiration stood out on his forehead.

'Will you people never understand?' he roared. 'My path is the true path to socialism. You are completely detached from the real world, you and all those like you. We are dealing with people who leave bombs in public places and blow the legs off children and old women. Where are their human rights? Why doesn't your precious committee come to Gazebo and talk to the victims? Why always listen to the refugees, the disaffected? What else do you expect them to say?'

'I tell you, Rosie ...' the General was towering over her as she sat cowering somewhat on the sofa, 'the only thing that my people really understand is fear. Fear is the most potent force in the world. I can get anyone to do anything to anyone through fear. Children will betray their parents and parents their children through fear. Fear is the ultimate weapon.'

'So you really believe that the war of ideas can be won by fear?' Rosie shot back.

'Yes.'

'And that you can gain control of the commanding heights of an economy through fear?'

'I'm sure of it.'

'The appeal has to be to the hearts and minds, Luis,' said Rosie.

The General began to breathe very heavily. 'Rosie, you are trying my patience. In the orderly room of the Royal Marines contingent there was a notice saying *Grab them by the balls and the hearts and minds will follow.* I like that. It's my kind of thinking.'

'That's fascist thinking, it's not the true path of socialism.'

'I've really had enough of this unrealistic posturing.' The General leaned down and grabbed Rosie by her wrists, jerking her onto her feet. He frogmarched her into the bedroom and taped her wrists to the end of the brass bedstead,. 'People like you make the world unfit for socialism,' he shouted, slamming the door as he went out. Rosie remained crying gently and tied up in the bedroom. In a few minutes Pedro came in and released her without saying anything.

***

Out in the countryside the partisans of Blue Fox were perfecting and improving their radio techniques. Wentworth Stringer had decided that the radio transmitters should be located some distance away from the Mulch ranch because he feared that the Mulch ranch was bound to be visited by Marranesian seaborne patrols sooner or later. Two miles inland from the ranch two adjacent crofters' cottages were situated. They were unoccupied, which was an advantage, and they were sturdy and watertight, as all buildings on the Islands had to be. They had the disadvantage that movements to and from them could be seen from Mount Longjohn, where it was safe to assume the Marranesians would have a lookout position. All movements to and from the cottages were therefore carried out after dark.

It was now ten days since Blue Fox and his small team had slipped out of Government House and about a week since they had learned on the radio that the Task Force had set sail. In rough rule of thumb terms, this meant about fourteen more days before the Task Force was off the coast of the Faraway Islands. Before then, however, those on the ground expected to see evidence of British air activity when they assumed the Port Roger airfield runway would be attacked.

The destruction of the C130 had been the most fabulous coup of the Blue Fox team. One lucky shot - for that was what it was - catching the aircraft at its most vulnerable on its final approach, had raised the 'partisans' to celebrity status in the Islands and cast a gloom over the Marranesians. Just as Rosie Long from her love nest in Government House sought to reassure the islanders that all was well, everything was normal, the Marranesians loved them and no British Task Force would be foolish enough to arrive — so Wentworth Stringer, alias Blue Fox, transmitted his news to the islanders, and his news was the destruction of the C130, the seizure of weapons at Huff Bay and news of the progress of the Task Force.

On islands where there was no mass media, truth and rumour chased each other round by means of telephone or short-wave radio. General Hernando knew that the *Blue Fox Team* consisted of three overweight British MPs playing soldiers and assisted by a Government House butler and some of his friends and relations, but to the islanders — particularly those living in Port Roger who had heard the C130 crash — a stick of British Commandos were operating on the Islands and this was very good for morale. Nor was the impact on the Marranesian forces insignificant. While the regular officers regarded Blue Fox with contempt, the ignorant, mainly teenage, conscripts were terrified by stories about the attack on Huff Bay. Two of the young soldiers who had been forced to load ammunition and equipment onto the Blue Fox boat at Huff Bay had had to be brought to Port Roger for medical treatment for ailments unrelated to the attack — one had a seriously cut hand and the other had influenza. They were visited in Port Roger Hospital by their friends and the friends listened in awe to the Huff Bay story and to how mighty the British were. These impressions were round all the conscripts within the same day.

Wentworth Stringer knew from his previous researches into the armed forces of Marranesia that the army rank and file were almost totally conscript and, moreover, they were conscripts from a society taught to fear rather than respect authority. While fear was a good motivator up to a point, if anything happened to the officer, the men would soon be looking for an opportunity to surrender. They had no wish to fight — let alone die — for a regime which they detested.

While Wentworth Stringer prepared further military forays against the occupying forces, he was also keen on the psychological warfare possibilities. He had disasessed such possibilities far into the night with Rollo and with Kelp. Rollo could speak passable Spanish. His parents had lived in Spain when he was a child and he had in adult life bought a villa in the Andalusian hills and went there often. Rollo reckoned that a short programme in Spanish could be broadcast each evening and that this programme would be aimed at the Marranesian conscripts. News of the approach of the Task Force and the incident at Huff Bay would have to be skilfully interwoven into some narrative.

Rollo had already worked out a rough narrative of folk stories of the Faraway Islands entirely made up by him and designed to exploit the superstition and gullibility of his audience. The real problem was going to be getting any sort of audience. The Marranesian conscripts were not, after all, endowed with individual transistor radios.

Kelp reckoned he had the answer. The key to success was to enlist the interest of the NCOs, who would almost certainly have some radios of their own and the way to do this was to have some talk about football. All Marranesians were crazy about the game and Kelp was confident that he could put together a short scrapbook-type piece that could be interesting. The hope would then be that the NCOs would ask some of the conscripts into their rooms to listen in. The remaining question was how to ensure that the NCOs knew about the programme. The Blue Fox team needed an immediate audience. They had no time for the slow build-up.

The plan centred on Mrs Patel, the denizen of Port Roger's *Island Commissariat*, a general purpose store. Despite her name, Mrs Patel was of Italian descent and had come, decades previously, to the Islands with her parents for a holiday. She had so fallen in love with the Islands that she returned some years later. She got to know Mr Patel, the owner of the main shop, whose father had been a butler for a previous Governor. The Patels were drawn together by a mutual lack of comprehension of the islanders, neither of them being of British stock.

It was this very unBritishness which Kelp believed could be an advantage. Already some of the officers and NCOs of the Marranesian forces were starting to frequent the stores. This non-Britishness of the Patels produced a form of unspoken alliance with those Marranesians who came their way.

Kelp telephoned one of his cousins in Port Roger, a cousin who he knew was on good terms with the Patels, and asked him to produce two or three handbills which were to advertise *Football Talk* on a particular wavelength every night at 21.00. Kelp asked the cousin to do what he could to chat up Mrs Patel — who had some knowledge of Spanish — to encourage her to draw the attention of her customers to the handbill. Kelp reckoned he was onto a winner because Mrs Patel loved to be chatted up as Mr Patel was hardly ever in the shop.

Kelp also included what marketing people would call the *launch incentive package*, by announcing on the handbills the day and date of the first transmission and the fact that there would be a quiz with prizes. Quiz entry forms would be available in the store to be returned to the store, but Kelp intended to keep the competition going long enough to ensure that the Marranesians were no longer around to claim the prizes.

In her Italian youth Mrs Patel would have sat out to take coffee or wine on the verandah outside the store. In the Faraway Islands of continuous wind, no-one sat out anywhere. Not to be completely outdone, Mrs Patel had created a *sitting in* section where customers could have a cup of tea or coffee or Bovril, which the islanders seemed to like.

The NCOs had more time on their hands than their men and were less briskly efficient than their officers so, just as Kelp had predicted, they were the group who stopped for coffee and read the handbills.

Kelp now had to work really hard to get his programme together and to do this he had to work closely with Rollo Herbert-Fitzherbert. As the two men sat at a plain table in the crofter's cottage drawing up their plans, they presented a considerable contrast. Where Kelp was tall, dark and panther-like in his lithe movements, Rollo was of average height, a bit overweight, with crinkly greyish hair and eyes that tended to water easily and stared rather a lot.

Kelp's football was to be the bait which attracted the listeners. The idea then was to have some news flashes — all of this in Spanish — and then to introduce the quiz. Some of the quiz questions would be at the end of the programme, following the football and also following a short story which Rollo was putting into serial form.

Rollo, as the Spanish speaker, had to do the lion's share of the work. In the football sequence he interviewed Kelp, who replied in English, pretending to be Bobby Moore, or Gordon Banks or Bobby Charlton. Rollo would then add a radio subtitle in Spanish by way of translation.

Rollo would then interrupt himself with a news flash describing the progress of the British Task Force and — in the first two broadcasts — recapitulating on the events at Huff Bay and the crashed C130.

In the second week of the broadcasts the news flashes included apparent interviews with British naval officers and pilots who could see the lights of Port Roger. It did not matter that Marranesian officers would scoff at such fabrications. They were not listening to the broadcasts, but some of their men were. And they believed every word of it. No-one ever tried to work out the size of the listening audience in the garrison, but it never needed to be very large — some tens or a hundred or two each night. They were, however, the ones who then spread the word. Despite what their officers and Red Rosie said, the British were coming and there was a British Commando unit already on the island.

Rollo was not finished when the football and news flashes ended. That was when he began his *Folk Tales of the Faraways*, describing himself as Father Felipe. He had enlisted Kelp's aid on the story line as Rollo found his non-existent creative juices were not functioning.

Rollo and Kelp agreed that any story had to involve sheep, of which there were huge numbers. The story was that the sheep contained the souls of the past deceased islanders who were condemned to roam the slopes until such time as they believed their deliverance was at hand. At such time they would come down to the sea. A plot was worked out with some power plays between the rival groups, but all looking forward to the eventual day of salvation. Rollo, who was no actor, attempted to develop the sort of confessional voice he imagined that Father Felipe would have.

Rollo and Kelp were not themselves entirely sure how they wanted the story to play out, but they recalled discussions with Wentworth Stringer at which there had been talk of encouraging the sheep down from the mountains and through the minefields which the Marranesians had laid. Any such action would, of course, have to be closely co-ordinated with the Task Force once they were ashore.

As Wentworth Stringer listened to Rollo and Kelp rehearsing their broadcasts in the next room, he thought what an extraordinary world this was. Here they were at the far end of the world playing at soldiers in a rather serious game and yet feeling very amateur, when all the time they should have been lolling in the smoking room or eating in the dining room or reading in the library. All the same, he would not have missed it for the world.

His adrenalin flowed so much and so often he almost felt sick at times, but he found that he had total recall of his army field training — how to use cover and move over broken ground, all that sort of thing. Once learned at a formative stage in his life, these lessons had never been forgotten. He cursed his lack of fitness and wished he hadn't had quite so many snifters in the smoking room, but he did walk a lot with his dogs when at home in Leicestershire so he was generally in quite good order. He wished that his wife was still alive. She had been killed in a car crash four years before and he knew she would have been thrilled for him in this adventure — as well as more than slightly concerned! His son was in the Scots Guards. Maybe he was in the Task Force. In any event, Wentworth Stringer hoped the old man wasn't causing his son too much embarrassment.

Apart from the special tingle that came from excitement, the dryness in the mouth at moments of danger and the exhilaration of success, the real delight had been the way the delegation had pulled together — everyone except Rosie, of course, and for her

Wentworth Stringer still felt a mixture of sadness and grim determination.

Rollo had been something of a revelation because he could be a very cantankerous so-and-so at the best of times — always ready with the question to the Cardinal on approved methods of contraception, that kind of thing. He had had some successes on the floor of the House, particularly when in Opposition, when he had single-handedly derailed a Government Bill on an abstruse point of procedure, but he was very much a loner and not on most lists of the people with whom one most wanted to be cast away. Nevertheless, here he was keeping his end up without complaint in the field and now doing these broadcasts in Spanish, which Wentworth Stringer thought were excellent.

The other revelation was Albert Blackhead. It was often said that it took a foreign trip to really get to know MPs in other parties and certainly on this trip the inner characters of each and every one were under scrutiny. Albert had been marvellous. Although he had fallen into every bog, stream, culvert and gully and off every jetty, boat and pontoon, he always came up for more and searched round for his trilby.

Albert had appointed himself the Blue Fox Quartermaster and he was busily employed trying to make a frame for a rucksack which would carry special supplies. The Mulch house was rich in tools but Albert had to try and work out what tools he would need for the following day so as to avoid having to move from the cottage to the house in daylight.

Albert worked on the kitchen table and by and large he could do most of the things he wanted to do. From time to time, however, a screwdriver would slip or he would drop a washer and then there would be an absence of expletives, only a soft *Botheration take it!* and then the gentle humming would resume.

Every evening after dark they went to the Mulch house to have supper until the time came for Rollo and Kelp to go back to the cottage and transmit the programme in Spanish. Wentworth Stringer's own broadcasts in English — with no fairy stories — were broadcast at noon and 1800 hours each day. If he was going to be away during the day, he would prepare a tape and show one of the Mulch family how to operate the machine.

As they all sat round the Mulch family table, Wentworth

Stringer reflected how lucky they had been, but also how effective too. They had no sentries out because they had no people spare who could be sentries and in any case they were insufficient in numbers to prevent a determined attack from succeeding. They did, however, feel reasonably safe in their assumption that the Marranesians were very unlikely to undertake a forced march over miles of boggy terrain in the dark. If they came at all they would use helicopters, in which case they would be heard; or they could come by sea to the Mulch jetty, in which case they would be seen.

If the door burst open and they were taken prisoner, or worse, the operation would still have been entirely worthwhile. They had the crashed C130 and Huff Bay as battle honours. They had boosted the morale of the islanders and started to dent the brittle morale of the Marranesians. In addition, they had generated a terrific team spirit and had tremendous crack in the process.

Nonetheless, Wentworth Stringer's agile mind was already working on the next military adventure. He raised the idea when the four were back at the cottage, not wishing to compromise the Mulch family by their knowing plans in case the Marranesians came to call. That General Hernando was not thought to be a very nice man.

'We'll have to have a go at another C130,' said Wentworth Stringer suddenly when they were all sitting on the spartan kitchen chairs. 'That last one we knocked out was a tremendous coup, but not so much in propaganda terms, because I think they were quite successful in putting it out that the plane crashed through pilot error. If another C130 were to 'crash' that would start to look really careless. The real point, of course, is the damage done to their supplies. They lost the lot on the C130, all their food, comforts and probably their mail. So we need another strike. What do you think, Kelp?'

Kelp began to talk, his features flushed with excitement. Several generations of intermarrying and a complete lack of contact with the outside world had not produced a population of Einsteins, but the islanders were not the retarded slow thinkers that British forces might take them to be when they arrived. Kelp had been educated to school leaving standard and then had been able to join a relative (everyone was a relative) in Government House. After some time he was able to progress through the staff ranks until the Governor before Mr Cunningham decided to take a risk and appoint him butler.

This had turned out well because Kelp was a good worker and not too proud to know he was still learning. His knowledge of the flora and fauna of the Islands was superb. Now he had his audience.

'I agree that a C130 is a good target. Since our last success they are flying in at night. In one way this is not so easy, in another way we have a chance.' He spread out a map of Port Roger and its airport on the table.

'All aircraft land from the east. Until the invasion aircraft never landed at night, so that the runway lights are temporary Marranesian ones which are switched on when planes are due and the lights are run off the control tower mains. The aircraft will approach first from the west and overfly the airfield. As it lines to approach for landing I can arrange for there to be a sudden blackout of all lights. By that time a pick-up truck will have driven out as the C130 starts its overflight along this road, which runs at an angle away from the airfield but is still roughly in line with where a pilot might expect to find a runway. The truck will put out on the road four or five sets of free-standing pre-lit storm lanterns in pairs up the road, the aim being to get the plane to land on the road. It's not as good as last time but it could cause a lot of damage.'

There was a silence for a moment, then Rollo spoke. 'What if the truck gets stopped?'

'Then the operation fails. It's a group of men in a pick-up truck with some lanterns. Hopefully they could talk their way out of it, but with all the lights having just gone out they could look very suspicious. It's a high risk and it's why I don't think you gentlemen should go on it. I think this is one for the Kelp family. These are our Islands, after all. I will want to go and set it up. I will go to ground in Port Roger afterwards for two or three days and come back by boat.'

'Sounds a capital scheme if you can get the times right,' said Wentworth Stringer.

'We'll have to practise it on a similar road somewhere else,' agreed Kelp. 'We won't have more than two minutes.'

Rollo and Albert agreed that it was worth a go and wished they could take part. Kelp said that the flights were probably going to be every other night so he ought to leave in one of the Mulch boats at first light. This was agreed and Kelp went to make arrangements with the family Mulch. Shortly before first light Wentworth Stringer, Rollo and Albert shook Kelp by the hand and he was away to the Mulch house and then to the jetty and on board. The fishing boats were regularly plying along the coast. The Blue Fox team settled down to their broadcasts and to await news of events.

Kelp had been right about the need to practise, but the real problem had been finding a stretch of road without attracting suspicion, and they concluded they could not. They then tried Kelp's uncle's yard and in the seclusion of this they could at least practise the offloading and manhandling of the lanterns. They managed to unload the whole sequence in 2 minutes 30 seconds, which Kelp thought might just do.

At seven in the evening the Kelps — three generations and two cousins, with old man Reuben Kelp in charge — took up position in the pick-up truck close to a disused warehouse. Kelp looked out for the plane on a slight promontory above a road junction. This was near the edge of town and after dark very few people were about. On that first evening the plane did not come. At half past nine Kelp stood everyone down for the night.

The following evening the Kelps again took up position. This time shortly after light Kelp saw the plane approaching. He gave the signal and the truck roared into life and drove to his position. He also sent a pre-arranged signal to his contact with his hand on the Control Tower generator: *Put out the lights*. Kelp jumped aboard and the truck set off towards the key road as the aircraft appeared overhead. The truck now went through the drills, stopping every fifty yards to unload pairs of lanterns and check that they were lit. Kelp was in the car of the truck controlling operations. As the aircraft started its turn, the last pair of lanterns was put in place and Kelp spoke on his mobile phone. At that instant everything was pitch dark. The aircraft lights above could be seen together with the rather weak lanterns.

The aircraft began its approach. Kelp held his breath. Maybe it would overfly and not try to land. He waited and the plane came lower and lower. The pilot clearly could see some lights — their lights! The plane was coming in. Lower and lower it came until the wheels clipped a stone wall and caused the nose to plunge. As the plane landed on the road, the port wing was torn off on one of the walls and the plane careered along with columns of sparks flying out underneath it. As the road turned slightly, there was a stone cottage and it was into this that the plane became finally embedded. There was no explosion. The truck had already fled back down the road before the aircraft touched the road and was now entering the outskirts of the town. Soldiers were now flashing lights and running on all sides. Some shots were fired. Kelp felt something hot and sticky on his hand. It was his father's blood.

Very quickly the truck reached the warehouse and a short detour was made to the Kelp home so that old man Kelp could be carried in. The truck was driven away and abandoned. Kelp picked up the phone to the Mulch farm and gave the agreed word from a selection of words to describe the outcome.

Ocelot meant that the plane had landed on the road. Wentworth Stringer and Rollo would now embellish that fact and get onto the airwaves within the hour. As Kelp returned to the room where his father lay, he realised just how high the price for success was going to be.

★★★

Over in Government House Rosie Long was discomfited in mind and in body. For once it was not blowing a gale, so she stood on the balcony and heard the C130 fly overhead. She was not ready for what she heard next — a series of muffled noises, not quite explosions but like a major accident. She also noticed that while she had been on the landing all the lights had gone out in the area and that this had, curiously, made everything quieter. This made the noises from the airfield all the louder. It sounded as though another C130 had crashed on approach — or what 'official version' would her General offer, she wondered.

Pedro entered with candles and returned her radio so that she heard the news flash in Spanish. Pedro translated it for her and she did not recognise Rollo's voice. At nine o'clock she heard Wentworth Stringer's voice as clear as a bell giving the news to the Islands of another blow to the Marranesians. Wentworth Stringer sounded so firm and so confident.

Something defiant stirred in Rosie and she asked Pedro to call the Duty Officer for a situation report cleared for her to broadcast in English. Red Rosie had to do her duty.

12

We are Panic-stricken

♦

In London, it had not been a good week for the Government. The media remained frustrated at their inability to be in every cockpit and every gun turret, thereby bringing the reality of war onto every domestic television screen. They were, however, not far away when HMS *Sodomite* was hit by Exocet missiles and lives were lost.

There were Statements in both Houses. Lord Mafeking made a short statement to the nation on television. It was sobering stuff: a necessary reminder of the price that had to be paid and of the uncertainty surrounding the whole enterprise.

There was criticism in some quarters of the impression given by Lord Mafeking on television. Whilst all agreed that it was an extremely difficult balance to strike, Lord Mafeking's expression and demeanour were so sombre as to make the public feel they were witnessing the first day of the Battle of the Somme, not a modern naval engagement in which the stricken vessel had not sunk.

The Prime Minister, however, had other concerns. For her, the Government's very survival was riding on the successful outcome of the conflict. In order to confound critics in the UK — in the House, in the Party, in the media — critics in the UN and EC, and critics in the US like the President and Admiral Legover, she had to have nothing less than a total, convincing victory, crowned by the unconditional surrender of the Marranesian forces on the Islands.

Nothing must be allowed to reduce or diminish the scale of the triumph which the Prime Minister was absolutely convinced would follow the landing of the Task Force. Her British boys would win, of that she was sure. There was just one problem. What happened if the Marranesians collapsed in a demoralised heap before the Task Force arrived? Intelligence interception of Marranesian internal transmissions indicated a tense, if not fragile, state of morale among the largely conscript force.

The real problem was that her admirable back bench colleagues Sir Wentworth Stringer and Rollo Herbert-Fitzherbert, with the unlikely support of Albert Blackhead from the Opposition benches, had slipped out of Port Roger following the surrender and had linked up with units of local resistance. Not content with that, they had formed a commando unit, started a radio station broadcasting in Spanish and English, and had led the Marranesians a merry dance. Transport aircraft had crashed, armoured cars had been shot up and weapons taken, and the whole of the Islands were agog that an SAS unit was already ashore. The trouble was that an SAS unit was not yet ashore. The Prime Minister called the War Cabinet together in her room behind the Speaker's Chair in the House.

The Prime Minister spoke first. 'Secretary of State for Defence, your situation report, please.' Lord Mafeking cleared his throat, but before he could speak the Prime Minister cut in.

'Or should we hear directly from the Chief of the Defence Staff? Do proceed, Admiral.'

Lord Mafeking was too relieved to feel slighted and, to be fair, the Admiral was there to brief the War Cabinet. Admiral Halliard, in uniform, stared at the Prime Minister.

'Prime Minister. Not good. *Sodomite* hit by Exocet. Fire damage. Thirty-eight killed. Task Force coming under air attack. Bombing raid on Port Roger airfield inconclusive.'

There was a pause. It became clear that CDS was not going to add anything unless he had to do so. Questions began.

'How long until the Task Force can get ashore?' asked the Prime Minister.

'Eight days at the earliest, Prime Minister,' replied CDS.

'Can the Sea Harriers hit targets ashore yet?' asked Woodcock.

'Yes,' replied CDS.

'Have they yet done so?' pressed Woodcock.

'Yes, on two occasions,' replied CDS.

'Really, CDS, do I have to ask for every detail? Could you please tell the War Cabinet how effective has been the use of the Task Force's most potent asset — its embarked air strike?'

CDS coughed. There was a pause.

'Neither mission was completely successful, Prime Minister.'

'Why not?'

'The targets were not where they were supposed to be, Prime Minister.'

'How not?'

'They had moved, Prime Minister.'

'Were any bombs dropped, CDS?'

'No point, Prime Minister. No targets. No bombs.'

'And that is how you describe a mission as not being completely successful?' returned the Foreign Secretary.

'Quite so, Foreign Secretary.'

'CDS, how would you assess Marranesian morale?' asked the Foreign Secretary, conscious that he had first look at the intelligence reports before even the Prime Minister saw them.

'Morale is low, Foreign Secretary,' said CDS.

'Why do you think that is?' asked the Prime Minister sharply.

'Largely conscript army. Far from home. Brutal officers.'

'Anything else which might be affecting morale?' the PM again.

'Disruption, Prime Minister,' replied CDS.

'Ah ha. Go on, CDS.' PM on the scent.

'Local resistance putting up a fight, Prime Minister.'

'CDS, have you ever heard of an MP called Sir Wentworth Stringer?'

'Yes, Prime Minister.'

'Where is he now?'

'On the Faraway Islands, Prime Minister.'

'Doing what?'

'Leading a local resistance unit, Prime Minister.'

'To what effect?'

'Transport aircraft C130 has crashed, although that may have been pilot error. Armoured vehicles destroyed. Weapons taken, Prime Minister.'

'Anything of a propaganda nature, CDS?'

'Yes, Prime Minister. Sir Wentworth broadcasts in English to the islanders. Code name Blue Fox. Good for morale. Tells them Task Force on way. His colleague — '

'Rollo Herbert-Fitzherbert,' the Chief Whip helpfully.

'Yes — is broadcasting in Spanish to the Marranesian troops.

Very skilful. We translate. Very clever. Weakens conscript morale.'

'Any other broadcasting going on?' Woodcock believed in the old adage, never ask a question unless you already know the answer. There was a pause. CDS looked uncomfortable, or rather, more uncomfortable than usual.

'CDS?' the Prime Minister quizzically.

'Yes, Prime Minister. There are broadcasts to the islanders in English given by someone called Red Rosie. She is ....'

'Yes, CDS, we know who she is, thank you,' said the Prime Minister dryly. 'I must ask the Lord Chancellor if treason is still a capital offence. A public execution in front of Transport House would do wonders for us in the opinion polls.'

Lord Mafeking stirred uneasily. He could never be sure when the Prime Minister was joking, as a sense of humour was not her strong point and, as his own sense of humour was somewhat rudimentary, he struggled when witticisms began flying about. To be on the safe side he jotted '*Transport House*' on his notepad so that he could find out where it was and then avoid it, just in case.

'CDS.' The Prime Minister cleared her throat. 'We need to co-ordinate these resistance activities — laudable as they are — with the landing of the Task Force. We do not want any accidents. Any "friendly fire" incidents. That would be deplorable.'

'Especially in the marginal seats,' said the Chief Whip *sotto voce*.

'Do you have a plan, CDS?'

'No, Prime Minister.'

'Why not?'

'We had made no allowance for activity by units of local resistance, Prime Minister.'

'I can understand that you would not have done so originally, CDS, but we have been getting intelligence reports now for over a week, nearly twelve days in fact, of this very vigorous activity. We must avoid friendly fire.'

'Yes, Prime Minister,' said the Admiral stiffly. Lord Mafeking was relieved that CDS had not brought his usual selection of toys with him. After the last time he had done so, a discreet message had been passed from the Cabinet Secretary to the Permanent Secretary at the Ministry of Defence that the War Cabinet did not need to be treated as children.

Even Roger Woodcock was taken in by the Prime Minister's apparent concern for the welfare of the trio of MPs acting in a heroic but unsustainable manner and what might happen when the Task Force arrived and began bombarding Marranesian positions on the Islands. To an extent, their concern was genuine. Although the Prime Minister had already decided where she would sit to watch Rosie Long's execution, she was very keen to see the Three Musketeers safe and well.

She had, however, an agenda of her own. How could she stop Blue Fox from continuing his activities, which at the present rate would bring the Marranesian garrison to its knees before the Task Force could fire a shot? She could not make that objective public even to the War Cabinet because a premature collapse of the Marranesians to them would be good news as it would avoid any risk of casualties to the Task Force. The campaign was now launched and needed a British military assault to conclude it in triumph.

'How soon will we have contact with Blue Fox, CDS?'

'Current plans. SAS unit ashore today. Contact very soon, Prime Minister,' replied CDS.

Lord Mafeking was never sure why he did it, but somewhere in the Mafeking family genes there was a small streak of impetuosity, otherwise describable as an inability to keep one's own counsel. This was the juncture in the discussion when he felt impelled to intervene.

'Prime Minister. Is it not the case that the sites chosen for the Task Force landing are in the north and north west of the Islands and are therefore some distance away from where Blue Fox was last active? If Blue Fox is going to concentrate his efforts on demoralising the garrison by hit and run tactics and most of the garrison is in the south, is there really such a danger of friendly fire at this stage?'

Actually this was a perfectly fair point and produced some nods around the table, until, that is, the nodders saw the Prime Minister's expression and froze mid-nod. The expression was all too clear. The blue eyes fixed Lord Mafeking like a rabbit in the headlights. Inwardly she seethed. Here she was, bidding fair to be one of the greatest political leaders of the century, embroiled in a challenge that was to establish her reputation as the greatest leader since Churchill, and she had been caught by having a complete dunderhead, an absolute nincompoop, in the key post in her Government. The worst of it was that it was all her fault. She had appointed him. It had all seemed so harmless when the Leader of the House of Lords, Johnnie Mollusc, had suggested that, now that the Defence Review had been completed and accepted, it would be helpful, in the light of various changes he thought would be useful in the House of Lords, if another senior Cabinet post could go to a Peer. He had proposed Arthur Mafeking. After a weekend to think it over several times she had agreed, although all her instincts were against. Her instincts should have been trusted.

'The problem with your analysis, Secretary of State, is that it does not take into account the fact that at this precise moment we do not know the location of Blue Fox. Moreover, he does not know our aims and intentions. We therefore face the inevitability of two elements on the same side but operating in an uncoordinated manner in the same theatre — contrary, so I have always been advised, to all the precepts of war. I believe that my earlier comments and requests still stand.'

The Prime Minister waited to see if there should be a response to her statement. There was none. She resumed.

'It is urgent that an SAS unit gets ashore, gets in contact with Blue Fox and gives him the means so that we can get into direct contact. We must speak to him. CDS, you will report as soon as the SAS link-up has been made. When we have that information, Foreign Secretary and Defence Secretary will liaise to ensure we can speak.'

Everyone was clear that *we* was decidedly royal and nothing else was envisaged. The Prime Minister wished to speak to Blue Fox herself. The War Cabinet meeting was over and the participants gathered their papers and left with a minimum of what might be general conversation.

★★★

The telephone rang on Jolyon's desk and Jolyon looked away from the text of a speech for Lord Mafeking to pick up the receiver. It was the Private Secretary of the CDS with the news that an SAS unit was ashore in the Faraway Islands and that contact had been made with Blue Fox. The way was now clear to arrange the speaking contacts with the Prime Minister. Jolyon thanked him and rang off. Without putting down the telephone, he put a call through to his opposite number at the Foreign Office, the Foreign Secretary's Private Secretary, Walter Boosey.

'Walter, it's Jolyon. I've just heard from CDS's office that an SAS unit is ashore and they are in contact with Blue Fox. You and I are now to set up the PM to Blue Fox link-up. The Chief of Defence Intelligence has given me a name and a phone number. But as these people come under your Department, I wondered if it would be better if you called him?'

'No, that's fine,' replied Walter. 'I'll call him at once. What name and number?'

'The number is 218 1644 and the name is Kevin.'

'Is that all? Just Kevin?' asked Walter.

'That's what I've been given,' replied Jolyon.

'They must be going through a "let's get informal" kick. I'll call you back.'

Half an hour later the two met at the corner of King Charles Street and Whitehall and walked round the corner into Parliament Square and then past the Queen Elizabeth II Conference Centre into Victoria Street and to their destination close to the intersection with Strutton Ground.

'Here we are,' said Walter as they approached a row of shops, including one selling artists' materials and doing picture framing.

'Are they above the shop?' asked Jolyon.

'No, they are the shop — and forget I said that,' replied Walter and winked.

Walter opened the shop door and they entered a shop seemingly crammed with paintings, most with labels attached, and various stands of artists' materials. Behind the counter a cheerful Sloane Ranger asked if she could help.

'We have an appointment with Kevin,' said Walter.

'You must be Mr Boosey from the Foreign Office with a colleague,' she said.

'I am.'

'Please come through.'

The Sloane led the way along a short passage past an office where what looked like invoices were being typed, and then into a light, airy room which had various paintings on easels and was clearly a form of studio. There were some upright high-backed chairs towards which the Sloane waved a languid hand.

'Do please sit down. Kevin will not be long.' They sat down and the Sloane left.

'I wonder what his real name is?' asked Jolyon quietly.

There was no time for Walter to comment. The door opened and in came Kevin. Kevin was short, slim, dark-haired, wearing a bow tie and brown corduroy jacket, and he advanced into the room behind a welter of hand movements before greeting each of his visitors with a double handshake. To Walter he said, 'Boosey is quite a name for someone in the FO, isn't it, ducky?' and to Jolyon, 'The name really is Kevin, my dear. How is your mother, by the way?' Jolyon was taken aback.

'She's improving. How did you know she had been ill?'

Kevin made some 'ah'-like sounds and tapped the side of his nose to indicate a sort of omniscience.

'Now then, my dears,' said Kevin, sitting himself opposite Walter and Jolyon. 'Are you post-impressionists or are you after Holbein?'

'Neither,' replied Walter. 'We want to commune rather urgently, in fact today. We speak on behalf of Sunflower Maxima.'

'Oh Lud, then we must not hang about. Sunflower's needs override all else,' said Kevin with a flourish. 'Communing is the province of my colleague, Kevin. He will join us.'

'Another Kevin?' asked Jolyon weakly.

'Yes, and why not? It's a super name. He wouldn't change and I wouldn't change. So I'm Kevin One and he's Kevin Two. If you'd been a habitué, you would have asked for me as Kevin One when you arrived, but you didn't. We were listening to you. We could even hear you in the street outside. It's amazing what some people say about us. It can be quite gorgeous, actually. Here's Kevin Two.'

In came a younger, taller, man with fair hair and a steady gaze. Kevin One did the introductions. 'This is Kevin Two. Picture framer by day, Zen Buddhist by night and short stop for Regent's Park Strollers on Sunday mornings. He's fast, he's flexible and he has a fabulous physique.' Kevin Two continued to gaze steadily. Walter was slightly amused but Jolyon felt that he had come home. He had to know more.

'You run a business from here?' asked Jolyon.

'Of course we do, ducky. Why do you think we have a shop? Not much point in having a shop unless it pays for itself. The Treasury would have our whatsits off in a flash if it didn't pay its way. If you had some paintings that you wanted framing or re-framing — say if your mother went into a home — you could bring them to us. Davina is very good at the front of the shop and we have a place in Southwark which does the work.'

'But that isn't the full extent of your work, surely?' probed Jolyon.

'Well it is and it isn't, ducky,' said Kevin One, raising his right index finger to make a point. 'I know what you're getting at. Let me begin at the beginning. The firm I work for, that is to say the holding company, not this wholly-owned subsidiary of a shop, is engaged in the business of knowing lots and lots about our foreign friends. The way we do this is to be as clever as we can be here in London. They know that we're doing it so they are looking to find people who are part of or who visit Government Departments. They know about both of you. Career details, photographs, mother's health, sexual peccadilloes, everything. We have a contract with the Department of the Environment to conserve the paintings in all Government buildings. We have a reason to be everywhere. We even act as sub-contractors in some foreign embassies. Can you imagine that?' Kevin One paused for effect.

'Of course, it's Kevin Two who does all the real work, the real comms work. Receivers in loo seats and loo rolls. It's amazing what people say in bathrooms, particularly if they think no-one is listening. Fountain pens, garden rollers, pictures, mirrors, Kevin Two has done it all. He will make the arrangements for Sunflower Maxima to have her talk. Won't you, Kevin?'

'Yes, Kevin,' said Kevin Two. 'I have already put in hand the arrangements for the two-way link-up. A message will be sent by secure means at 13.00 hours to each of you. The link-up will begin at 15.30 with briefing *in situ* at 15.00.'

'Where will the briefing be?' asked Walter.

'You will be told at 13.00. Please follow the instructions to the letter.' Kevin Two resumed his steady gaze.

'We're very grateful to you both,' began Walter.

'Indeed we are,' chimed in Jolyon.

'The pleasure is all ours, I can assure you,' gushed Kevin One. 'It's so good to meet some real people instead of listening to tapes and decrypting code all day. If Elliott Ness was the Untouchables, I feel we are the Unmentionables. Every country needs us, but won't admit they have us. We are completely invisible ...' Walter and Jolyon thought for a moment that Kevin One was going to break down and cry, but he suddenly turned to Kevin Two, who was sitting alongside him with a side table between them, and said, 'But we'll show them, Kevin Two.'

'You bet, Kevin One.' And with that they immediately arm-wrestled, with Kevin One beating him of the fabulous physique.

Not sure quite what they would see next, the two officials stood up as one and Walter spoke first.

'I think we'd better get back to wait for instructions.'

'Very well. Nice to meet you.' Kevin One gave them the double handshake again.

Kevin Two said, 'See you this afternoon and follow the dress code strictly.' He smiled.

A moment later and Walter and Jolyon were back in busy Victoria Street, the world of picture framing behind them.

★★★

At precisely 13.00 sealed instructions arrived at the Foreign Office and the Ministry of Defence. They could only be opened by Walter and Jolyon once they had identified themselves to the messenger. They rang each other at once. They were equally incredulous. 'I thought we'd be going onto the roof of Admiralty House or something wild like that, or even Joint Headquarters at Northwood, but this, this is wild,' said Jolyon.

'I agree,' said Walter. 'But at least you don't have the challenge which I have of briefing Number Ten. Sunflower Maxima does not like leaving the office at all, let alone dressing up when she gets there.'

'I'll see you at the briefing then. I hope we have some nice dinky overalls. Powder blue would be nice,' said Jolyon.

'That's quite enough of that,' retorted Walter. The picture framers had clearly got to Jolyon.

The instructions — each of which was different for each Cabinet Minister attending the link-up — called for the Minister and Private Secretary to be taken by car to different streets around the Science Museum in South Kensington.

Jolyon and Lord Mafeking were taken by 14.45 to a small road between the Science Museum and Imperial College. There a Portacabin had appeared as well as a small canopy over an underground grating. Inside the Portacabin were two officials who handed over overalls and hard hats. The overalls were dark blue and the hard hats were yellow. Sizes had been notified in advance, so the pair looked reasonably business-like as they were led to the canopy which covered the open grating and then down a metal fixed ladder and onto an underground walkway. The two men were to follow an official clad in overalls and hard hat also, and his task was to lead them the half mile or so distance to the rendezvous.

At the same time the Prime Minister, grumbling about the size of her overall coat and her hard hat, was being led to the rendezvous, as were the Foreign Secretary and the Chief Whip, each accompanied by a Private Secretary to ensure that they arrived.

The rendezvous, when everyone had ascended to street level again, was a hollowed-out builder's skip situated in Queen's Gate Place Mews. Although hollowed out, the skip had its own integral roof structure of metal and canvas, onto which plenty of rubble had been heaped to give it a genuine look. A door had been cut in the side with a sliding door inside it to increase security and sound-proofing. Inside, the lighting was good and there were sufficient chairs for the size of group. At the far end of the skip was a table housing the radio sets. In front of the table stood Kevin Two, who had greeted the Prime Minister and each Minister as they entered and shown them to a seat.

Kevin Two began the briefing on time at 15.00. He showed on a map where Blue Fox was and pin-pointed some of the main action items, including recent Blue Fox successes and the Task

Force landing zones. He then explained that a two-way radio had to be operated according to standard procedures and he outlined what those were. He took questions, and the countdown commenced at 15.30. The Prime Minister had been rehearsed on how to use the pressle switch, which she had to press when she spoke and release when not speaking.

Precisely at 15.30 Kevin Two transmitted, 'Hello, Climax One.' (Blue Fox's call-sign for the Task Force). 'Climax One. This is Jezebel One Zero.' (Did they *mean* Jezebel? wondered Jolyon. Who chose these call signs anyway?) 'How do you read me? Over.'

There was a short pause and then loud and clear Blue Fox himself. 'Hello, Jezebel One Zero. Jezebel One Zero, this is Climax One. You are loud and clear. How me? Over.'

Kevin Two again. 'Climax One, Climax One. Sunflower Maxima will now speak to you.' There was a pause as the Prime Minister pressed the unfamiliar pressle.

'Hello, Wenty dear.' Silence.

Kevin Two quietly, 'You must say '*Over*' or he thinks you have something else to say.'

'How confusing. Over to you, Wenty, over, dear.'

This time a reply. 'Jezebel One Zero. Delighted to hear your voice, Sunflower Maxima. This is Climax One. We are in good heart and send greetings, over.'

'Hello, Climax Wenty. We are delighted with what you are doing, over.'

'Jezebel One Zero, we have been quite busy and there is no sign of any let up as the Task Force approaches, over.'

'Climax One,' the Prime Minister was getting the hang of it now, 'would it not be a good idea to stop your campaign and co-ordinate with the Task Force? Over.'

'Jezebel One Zero, we are now co-ordinated with Special Forces and are integrated into their operation. We are about to take the upper hand. Your courage will be rewarded soon with victory, over.'

'Climax One, we are all proud of you. The country is proud of you and your colleagues. We salute you all. But we are anxious that you don't get hurt now, over.'

'Jezebel One Zero, very kind of you to worry about us but we have shown we can take care of ourselves. Shame to miss out on the party now. Your courage will be rewarded with victory. We salute you, our great leader, over.'

The Prime Minister flushed.

'Climax One, we look forward to your safe and early return. God bless you all, over and out.'

'Jezebel One Zero, thank you and we look forward to having a drink with you in Number Ten, over and out.'

As the Prime Minister retraced her steps from the hollowed out skip in Queen's Gate Place Mews along the underground gantry to her pick-up point, she regarded that conversation as a complete failure. There had been no way that she could separate the party interest from the national interest in so public a forum. She had still not given up on the idea and continued to fret over it and gnaw at it in her mind.

★★★

In the same week of the casualties on HMS *Sodomite* fell the decision on the future of the Marranesian battleship *Positano*. The huge, but outdated, battleship had been detected by a Royal Navy submarine and a request had been sent back to London for clarification of the rules of engagement.

The debate in the War Cabinet ran along predictable lines. The Foreign Secretary, who, until the very landing of the Task Force, hoped that the Marranesians would recognise the inevitable and surrender, viewed any action which could increase intransigence as counter-productive. As the Positano was reported to be sailing away from the newly established exclusion zone, he could see propaganda advantages in not sinking her.

Once again in this type of debate, the Prime Minister found herself in total accord with her Defence Secretary, whose instincts were as good as his judgment was not. He simply asked who it was we were going to fight. If we were not to bomb Marranesia itself, as far as he was concerned any warship which put to sea was putting itself in jeopardy. It was as simple as that. These were the Prime Minister's sentiments entirely. CDS agreed that the deed could be done. The order to sink the Positano was sent.

That would have been the concluding item on the War Cabinet

agenda, but the Prime Minister had one other item under *Any Other Business.*

'Colleagues will recall my concern at our last meeting at the dangers of losses through friendly fire if we fail to co-ordinate Blue Fox and the Task Force. Some of you heard my radio exchange with Blue Fox earlier today and it was clear there was no way I could get him to ease back on his planned programme. So important do I believe this issue to be that I am asking the Secretary of State for Defence to fly out and join the Task Force forthwith so that he can carry my personal message to Wenty.'

There was a gasp of astonishment round the table. The Prime Minister had mentioned it briefly to Lord Mafeking before the meeting but he did not think she meant it. He thought it best to give a forced smile and to say simply, 'I will do my best, Prime Minister.'

'I think we should congratulate the Defence Secretary on his courage and wish him Godspeed,' said the Foreign Secretary, and they all said 'Hear, hear,' and banged the table in approval.

'CDS will make the arrangements, Defence Secretary, but do come and see me before you go.'

The War Cabinet meeting closed and the Prime Minister smiled inwardly. By this stratagem she had a chance of Wenty getting the political message when no other chance existed; she would focus public opinion on her Government in support of our gallant services; she got out of the way a Government figure who was consistently best in public opinion approval ratings. Nonetheless, there were lingering doubts. She was sending an unguidable missile into a war zone; but surely there was nothing he could do to snatch defeat out of the jaws of victory — surely.

13

A Bubble Reputation

♦

No-one could ever recall exactly how it came about that Lord Mafeking was allowed to join the Task Force. Some with claims to greater powers of recall said that Lord Mafeking had simply told the Prime Minister that he had to do it and she was too dumbfounded — for once — to object. It was, of course, entirely without precedent and could not possibly be allowed, said officials, advancing the very arguments guaranteed to ensure the failure of their case.

The conundrum that faced the Defence Chiefs was as follows. The Task Force had by now sailed beyond the range of land-based aircraft, unless those aircraft could be refuelled in the air, and this was not done for the slower carrier on board delivery aircraft. The only way in which key personnel or supplies could reach the Task Force was to parachute them into the sea alongside the ships.

The First Sea Lord was appalled. Commander in Chief at Northwood was appalled. The Commander of the Task Force was appalled, but they all had to get on with it and get it done. No-one said it could not be done, but there was no getting away from the significant element of risk.

Lord Mafeking and Jolyon, the ever-present Private Secretary, were to make the jump. On the aircraft from Brize Norton to Whitsun Island they were briefed and briefed and briefed again as to the procedures. Again, when the C130 left Whitsun to find the Task Force they were briefed and rehearsed.

It was at Whitsun that Jolyon made his first major announcement. He came out in the crew room. As the crews hurried about their tasks, checking routings and so on, Jolyon was in the locker room putting the final touches to his wet suit. When he emerged from the locker room, Jolyon caused all work in the crew room to stop. Everyone stared. Jolyon had put an outsize bra over his wet suit and what could only be described as a ballet skirt at his waist. After a pause the crew room burst into applause to salute a brave gesture from a brave man.

Lord Mafeking entered at that moment and he too was taken aback but he nonetheless appreciated at once the significance of Jolyon's attire.

'My gosh, Jolyon. You're a poofter.'

'That's right, Secretary of State. A poofter.'

'And a very brave one too,' said Lord Mafeking, almost tenderly.

It was time for the mission to begin.

The embarked media on the Task Force were in a very invidious position. They were very close — maybe too close — to what threatened to be front-line action, but their only means of communicating with their hungry news editors was controlled by the Royal Navy and they all had no choice but to accept the homogenised product put out to all by the Task Force spokesman.

On this day they knew that someone special was coming to join the Task Force but who it was they were not told. Photographs were allowed and after an interval of 24 hours they were permitted to be sent. By then the operation had gone smoothly — Lord Mafeking was now assuming the cult status of a war hero back home in the media; no-one had noticed anything unusual in the contraption around Jolyon's middle, although Jolyon swore it gave him greater buoyancy in the water. The Admiralty Board later denied that ballet skirts were to be mandatory for all flights over water.

Only in one respect had the operation not been a complete success. On entering the water the batteries of Lord Mafeking's hearing aids had been ruined and the spare set had fallen into the sea. This incident was to have profound consequences later.

For the moment, though, Lord Mafeking could not have been in better form. Jolyon was on hand to pass on requests and messages in both directions and, unlike many deaf people, Lord Mafeking became more benign with increased deafness. This was probably fortunate at this juncture because less than twelve hours after coming on board, the Task Force was attacked by the Marrancsian Air Force as it entered Groin Bay.

Lord Mafeking noticed plumes of water rising in the bay and felt the ship shudder, but noise-wise it was all rather peaceful for him. Jolyon asked him to put on a helmet.

★★★

In the War Cabinet skip in Knightsbridge the Prime Minister could see her worst fears coming true. General Hernando might want to do a deal with Wentworth Stringer which would be made to look as though the General had graciously acceded to the islanders' wishes and withdrawn without having to surrender to the Task Force — particularly if Wenty was mad enough to accept his surrender. To make matters worse, Lord Mafeking was now the toast of the country and anyone would think it was his Task Force. Why on earth did she ever agree to his going? The Task Force Commander would have to accept the Marranesian surrender. She could feel a victory parade coming on — in both Port Roger and the City of London — and made a note to her Private Secretary to start the wheels turning.

It had been arranged that a three-way patch up would take place on the radio, but if one of the participants is deaf the arrangement can only work if someone on the line writes out the questions very quickly for the deaf person. Jolyon was to do this. Lord Mafeking's condition had been explained to the Prime Minister and to Wentworth Stringer, who was now operating close to Port Roger and no longer feared discovery from Marranesian forces.

The Prime Minister had mastered the radio procedure now with her *Over* and *How do you read me?* but the first few exchanges were devoted to everybody saying hello and that they were there.

'Arthur,' said the Prime Minister direct to Lord Mafeking, 'I must congratulate you on your courage. You are a national hero now.' There was a pause as Jolyon scratched out the message for Lord Mafeking.

'Thank you, Prime Minister,' said Lord Mafeking with a fair degree of boom but not too much. He then decided to go on to transmit in every sense of the word.

'Prime Minister. I'm very lucky to be in one piece but I am — and the Task Force is — in very good heart and everyone is very

147

loyal to you. We're going ashore soon and we'll have to account for these fellows. Then we'll take the surrender. Credit to Blue Fox, who has done a wonderful job, but he won't want to be taking the surrender. He's not the man for it, protocol demands it is properly done, he knows it and you need have no worries on that score.' He stopped. When the Prime Minister was sure he'd stopped she felt very gratified and then asked Wentworth Stringer if he had heard the Secretary of State.

'Certainly did, Prime Minister. Completely agree. No place for us irregular chaps on these occasions.'

After further exchanges of a cordial and congratulatory nature, the network closed and the Prime Minister felt a great deal of satisfaction. The surrender would be taken by the Task Force and she would then need to fly in soon thereafter. She must take another look at that flak jacket she was given by the Guards last year.

★★★

Blue Fox lost no time in taking to the air and announcing that the Task Force landings had begun and that the clock was now ticking for the Marranesian occupying forces. Rollo too from the same safe house on the edge of Port Roger announced in Spanish that the British Task Force had landed and that among them were units of the Special Air Service noted for cannibalism.

Rollo then switched to his regular early evening series of talks from Father Felipe. The good Father had been talking each time about folk tales from the Faraway Islands and tonight was to be the *pièce de résistance*.

Father Felipe described how when people in the Faraway Islands died their souls could not get to heaven because it was too far and God's chariot only called once in a while to gather up souls. In the meantime the souls took refuge in the sheep and whenever there was a national crisis and the Islands were in danger, the sheep would rise up and sort out the trouble.

To sophisticated western ears this sort of stuff was preposterous, but one had to remember that the Army of Marranesia was very largely conscript. Intelligent, well-educated

Marranesians avoided the draft. The ranks were filled with ignorant, illiterate and superstitious country boys. Rollo had been clever in mixing in items about football (their great love), a little news with a propaganda twist, weather news from home (which he fabricated) and then a story from Father Felipe. The whole programme was no more than 30 minutes and it was timed at 17.00 hours when most of the men were resting and the Corporals, in return for a few cigarettes, would let the men listen to their radios. The Corporals affected bravado and military discipline, but just below the surface they were as superstitious as the country boys.

On the evening of the landings, Rollo reported the landings in a very matter of fact way, adding other items of world news — now old — which he had got from the Mulch family radio. Nonetheless the message went home in the minds of the conscripts as they returned to rotate front-line duties in the dug outs and trenches around Port Roger and which faced the mountains.

Kelp and Rollo had been working out a scheme and Kelp was about to put it into practice. It had been agreed that Rollo would do a series of Father Felipe stories to establish the pattern and the confidence in the listeners. It was agreed that on the evening of the announcement of Task Force landings Father Felipe would give the 'sheep with the souls of the departed' story.

Kelp had arranged with the shepherds of the mountain flocks that the victorious British Government would compensate them for any loss of sheep, if they were prepared to drive their flocks down the mountain towards Port Roger.

There were tens of thousands of sheep on the mountains overlooking Port Roger that evening. Some people described it as an extraordinary act of warfare in any era as the sheep at a given agreed time began to move towards the town. As they came on they entered the minefields and began to detonate the mines.

The explosions attracted the attention of the troops in trenches at the edge of town. The mountain looked like a sea of white moving steadily, despite the intermittent explosions, towards the staring conscripts.

Father Felipe's story had been heard by lots of the young soldiers and they quickly told their colleagues as the sheep advanced. For what seemed like ages no-one did anything. The officers were surprised and suspected a trap of some sort — a diversionary tactic perhaps. It was rather a different form of diversion, aimed at nothing less than the morale of the Marranesian forces.

Sheep are about as harmless an animal as one can find, unless perhaps a flock is closing in on food. But if people believe that the sheep are imbued with spirits from the past, then anything can happen. A young Lance Corporal stood up and let out a cry of dismay. At once others sprang out of their trenches and began running for the Barracks in the town. Officers fired shots in the air but even they were disconcerted as the troops began to fall back and head for the only security they could imagine in their Barracks. Kelp was following events through his binoculars and was very pleased by what he saw. The Marranesians were becoming a rabble.

★★★

In Government House, where the detonating sheep were clearly audible, Rosie was surprised when an orderly appeared with a letter. She opened it. It read:

> *Dear Rosie,*
> *Your colleagues are near and want to meet you. Please accompany the man who gave you the letter. He will bring you to us.*
>
> > *Yours ever,*
> >
> > *W.S.*

Rosie stood up at once and nodded to the orderly. Together they went out of the front door and to the car which Rosie had for her exclusive use. The orderly told the driver to go to a certain address and the three of them drove off.

Presently the car arrived at a detached bungalow near the edge of town. The orderly and Rosie went inside and there were Wenty, Rollo and Albert. Their enmities dissolved at once. They were parliamentary colleagues again. Rosie was so pleased to see the Three Musketeers — as she called them to herself — looking so well. Their affection for her was heavy with sadness rather than anger. Blue Fox spoke first.

'It'll soon be all over, Rosie,' he said. 'You know the Task Force is ashore and the end is inevitable. We would like to see a cease fire to prevent further casualties. What do you think?'

Rosie had sat down in the middle of a circle of chairs facing the verandah and with their backs to the door.

'I would like to see a cease fire too, but what can I do to bring it about?' Rosie asked of the others, who were seated on either side of her. General Hernando had entered the room silently behind them.

'You can broadcast my terms to the British General for a start,' said the General from the door. The delegation leaped to their feet and turned round in shock to see the General. Blue Fox shot an angry glance at Rosie, suspecting that she had brought the General, but the General saw the glance and waved a hand.

'This is not the work of my Red Rosie,' said the General with some remorse as he advanced into the room. 'I knew that you three would want to contact Rosie sooner or later and my D/F locator tracked you to a house in this street. All I then had to do was position two vehicles in the street and have them alerted whenever Rosie went out in her car. The house is surrounded and the entire garrison will prevent any escape or rescue. You are my prisoners.'

'Brilliant. Absolutely bloody brilliant.' Albert almost startled himself with his outburst. Blue Fox was icy.

'I suppose you are in touch with events in the Islands, General?'

'I am aware that your Task Force is being attacked by heroic units of the Marranesian Air Force in Groin Bay,' retorted the General.

'Actually your Air Force is behaving heroically — full marks to them. They are fighting well,' Blue Fox said.

The General was taken aback. 'How can you say that?'

'Because I saw the attack in Groin Bay. I also saw the Task Force come ashore and I met the Commander, Major General Wallop. He gave me this message for you, General.'

Before the General opened the letter he asked Blue Fox, 'But the attacks were yesterday at Groin Bay, which is over eighty miles away — probably three days' march.'

'You're right, General, but I didn't march. Not at my age. Our Special Forces took out your Huff Point base plus the helicopter some days ago. We have been on your net, using your call-signs, in perfect Spanish of course. They brought me here.' He paused. 'Would you like to read General Wallop's letter now?'

General Hernando's face was a study of shock and disbelief as he opened the letter. He had been told that the sheep detonation of mines was simply bomb throwing practice. His staff were afraid to describe the virtual disintegration of morale in his troops because his temper was legendary. If the General did not know about the sheep he was smart enough to realise that if Blue Fox was able to operate as he now could, the game was effectively up.

General Hernando. I request that you order a cease fire at 10.00 hours on the morning after you receive this message. At that time we can make arrangements for the unconditional surrender of your forces to me. Blue Fox has my call sign and frequency. Major General Wallop.

General Hernando asked Blue Fox to give him the details and called into the corridor to get the radio equipment brought in from his vehicle. This took a few minutes, during which time no-one spoke.

A radio operator brought in the equipment. General Hernando noticed that Pedro, his valet, had also come in. He was about to ask what Pedro was doing when the radio became active and soon the two Generals were in direct contact. General Hernando was expected to respond. He did so.

'General Wallop. My compliments to you. Even you do not know the entire situation here in Port Roger. All the members of the British parliamentary delegation are here with me. They are safe and well, but they are my prisoners. I have certain demands and if they are not allowed, I cannot answer for the safety of the delegation.'

General Wallop replied in crisp, well-educated English tones. 'I would like to speak to Blue Fox, please.' Blue Fox went to the transmitter.

'Hello Magnet One Four, this is Blue Fox. I confirm that we are prisoners of General Hernando but only within the last hour has this happened.

This last piece of information was helpful for General Wallop, giving the impression of a hasty and ill-considered action on the part of General Hernando.

General Wallop spoke again. 'What do you ask, General?' General Hernando took a deep breath.

'First, I want to surrender my forces to Blue Fox, who has been instrumental in the collapse of morale in my forces. Second, I want to fly out to Marranesia with my immediate staff after the surrender to Blue Fox.' There was a pause and some interference on the line.

Then it was General Wallop again, even crisper and more terse than before. 'General Hernando,' he began. 'You are fully aware of your situation. Militarily you have to surrender. You will not be allowed to surrender to anyone other than myself. That is not open for discussion.'

'Second, my government in London has anticipated your request to fly out after the surrender and has expressly authorised me to grant that permission for you and your immediate staff.' The General paused, then continued, 'As for your remarks about the safety of the parliamentary delegation, you are as aware as I am about the Rules and Conduct of War in relation to the treatment of parliamentarians, even those who have chosen to take up arms against you. I require details of the safe whereabouts of all the parliamentary delegation one hour from now. When I am satisfied, the cease fire can be announced for 10.00 hours tomorrow, followed by your surrender to me at the Barracks at Port Roger at 12 noon. You may then fly out at 14.00 hours. Is that clear, General?'

There was a pause, quite a long pause, then General Hernando said, 'I accept.'

'Very well, General. I thank you for your acceptance. I shall expect a message from Blue Fox confirming the delegation's safety in one hour and after that broadcasts can be made to respective forces and to the Islands. Over and out.'

The room was suddenly very still. General Hernando spoke to Pedro. 'What are you doing here? Your place is in Government House, pressing my suits.'

'As a British agent,' said Pedro, 'my job was to be sure that you agreed to the cease fire and to kill you if you did not.' He produced his own gun and removed the General's gun from his holster. Pedro then motioned to the radio operator to get out, snarling something unpleasant to him as he went.

'The time has come, Rosie, for your Three Musketeers to leave. Pedro will show us the way. Will you come with us?' asked Blue Fox.

'No. I'll see you boys tomorrow.' — She shot a glance at General Hernando — 'At the Barracks at 12. Tell General Wallop I'm fine and I will be making my broadcast in an hour or two.'

Blue Fox, Rollo and Albert followed Pedro out and presently their car was heard driving off. Rosie and the General were alone.

'First my Red Rosie. Now even my valet is a British agent. How typically British — heads they win, tails I lose. I've had my balls shot off just as though it had happened in a trench.' The General was now morose, with flickers of the old defiance. Rosie was not sure what to say. She was so full of so many emotions she thought she might burst.

In a very short space of time she had been inspired by Marxist possibilities; infatuated and swept off her feet by a real Latin lover; shocked to discover his past; angered and bewildered by the ferocity of opposition to her from Wentworth Stringer, Rollo and Albert; worried nonetheless that they were going to be all right. She had taken on board the fact that men and maybe women from her constituency were sailing into danger and she had sided with the enemy. She was naturally a warm, loving, approachable and, above all, loyal woman. She felt that she could never really explain to those she cared for and cared about why she did what she did.

As for Luis, she was as certain as she could be that she still loved him. His very aggression and highhandedness were at once frightening and yet also inspiring and reassuring, like being led by a real man. There may even have been a streak of masochism in her make-up. In any event, she needed to know how he felt. She knew he was divorced, but she did not really know whether she was a 'campaign romance', soon forgotten when the medals are handed out — not that there would be many Marranesian medals after this shambles.

'Well, Rosie. I believe your expression is — say something, if it's only goodbye,' the General broke her reverie.

'Oh Luis, I have never been so confused and upset in my whole life.' He took her in his arms, which in itself was immediately comforting, and he kissed the back of her hair.

'I'm not exactly feeling on top of the world myself — leader of a military disaster which was launched by a military régime. No prizes for guessing who will be the Number One National Scapegoat. It would only be worse if I were Manager of the National Football Team and we had been knocked out of the World Cup.'

Luis sat Rosie down in an armchair and looked round the modest front room, taking in the photograph of the Queen above the mantelpiece, the George VI Coronation mug on the mantelpiece and a newspaper cutting of Princess Diana imperfectly framed on the sideboard.

'Who lives here?' asked Luis.

'I've no idea,' replied Rosie. 'The boys were using it as a safe house, I understand, for the last two or three days.'

'Well, they won't need to worry about safe houses much longer. The whole Islands will be safe for your boys.' He emphasised the last two words.

'What are you going to do, Rosie? Can you go back?' Luis wanted to know.

Rosie shook her head. 'I don't know, Luis. Politically I've been a fool, maybe. I've got in too deep. That happens. But emotionally and as a woman I've found you and that has been so special, even though you've hurt me and humiliated me. I can take it because I can understand you and where you are coming from. You and I are products of totally different cultures and political systems. Your answer to a bomb in Northern Ireland would be to blitz Dublin. I passionately disagree. I won't infuriate you by trying to persuade you that your ways don't win, at least not in the long term. Kill lots of people in the short term and the terror will rule, but in the end it always has to be a political solution, wherever it is.'

'I understand all that and disagree with you violently. You British are so sanctimonious,' replied Luis, but with a smile. 'Of course it will be difficult for you to go back at first, but your Prime Minister will get a great victory with parades. I would not be surprised if she is not already planning a parade in Port Roger.

She will not want to pursue you, surely. What is she going to do — have you tarred and feathered and whipped down Whitehall behind a Guards band? I don't think so. Of course it will be painful. Friends you thought you had will have turned against you. Some friends will be real friends, but above all you will be with your own people.'

He paused. 'What can I offer you? To accompany a disgraced military leader who might well be court-martialled and shot. You are a foreign Mata Hari figure who does not speak Spanish, who could be a widow within weeks.'

'A widow?'

'You would have to marry me.'

'Would I now?'

'It might produce a happy ending — but then it might not. That is quite the worst offer to set before a woman.'

'Let me be the judge of that.'

Luis crossed the room and took Rosie's hand. 'I think we should leave it like this. There is a place on my plane for you tomorrow as there is a place in my heart for you always. Tomorrow at the parade you will see your people in their military might. They are very professional, very skilful, some of the best troops and airmen in the world. I am giving in. I am surrendering to a courteous enemy, but an uncertain future. I want you to come with me but at that moment, at the end of the parade tomorrow, you must give me your answer. You owe it to yourself not to give me an answer now.'

Without a further word Luis escorted Rosie back to Government House.

★★★

Jolyon had had his arguments and battles with the Military back in the Ministry of Defence, where as a mere civilian he was barely tolerated. Here, however, in an operational context, he was agog with admiration for the sheer efficiency of the military infrastructure and backup systems. Here was everything that the modern army might need beyond the traditions of food, water and ammunition to mail, satellite dishes, laptop computers and even the common or garden battery source of power for so many items like torches and — of particular interest to Jolyon and Lord Mafeking — hearing aids. Jolyon was very keen to get his boss back 'on net' so that he could mingle with the troops and tell them how good they were. It was very rare to have a Secretary of State for Defence visiting troops in a 'hot' situation other than, say, Northern Ireland, which was a rather special case.

Lord Mafeking had been very well received by the troops, many of whom had seen his arrival from their various troop ships. He and Jolyon had now reached a line of artillery gun emplacements for the 105 mm guns situated on a hill where they commanded a view of the main approach to Port Roger.

Lord Mafeking and Jolyon were sitting in the Battery Commander's sandbagged dugout behind the guns being shown the maps. As he was to describe to the Ministry Inquiry later, Jolyon noticed out of the corner of his eye an RAF Chinook helicopter heading towards their position with a large container slung underneath. The Chinook was very much the supply officer's workhorse, carrying as it did very large quantities of supplies slung underneath in nets, as well as small armoured vehicles and soldiers inside.

In order to unload, the Chinook had developed a manoeuvre which brought it in a straight line low over the rear echelon positions, including that of the Battery Commander. The aircraft began its run, and it was always a noisy machine. On that day the noise seemed to bounce off the rocks and amplify. The usual response of most people is to duck slightly, as people do when walking towards a helicopter which has its blades circling.

No-one will ever know why Lord Mafeking chose that moment to stand up and, moreover, stare in the opposite direction to the approaching helicopter so that he did not see the Chinook, let alone hear it. Lord Mafeking may have seen Jolyon's screamed but inaudible warning, but before anyone could pull him to safety he was struck on the head by the underslung container and fell violently on his face. The Battery Medical officer certified that death was instantaneous and it was officially announced '*with great regret*' that '*in the hour of victory the Secretary of State for Defence, Lord Mafeking, had been killed in an accident near Port Roger.*'

Jolyon learned later that the spare replacement batteries for

Lord Mafeking's hearing aid were in the container which killed him.

★★★

Since first light columns of Marranesian soldiers had been lining up to place their weapons in a pile in front of the Barracks armoury. As nearly 10,000 Marranesian troops were involved, this had proved to be a considerable logistical exercise, as the men stacked their weapons and ammunition in designated piles.

One problem facing the Task Force for the surrender ceremony was that the parade ground was far too small to accommodate all potential participants, there not having been much need for military ceremony in Port Roger in the past. The order from the Task Force Commander to General Hernando was that in addition to 3,000 men, all officers and NCOs were to be on parade to witness the surrender. Spanish-speaking British officers went to ensure liaison and that everyone attended who should attend.

Wentworth Stringer was now wearing his blazer, complete with regimental badge which Pedro had saved for him and hidden in Government House. He really looked every inch the distinguished, if rather weather-beaten, Knight of the Shires once again and not someone on the way to audition for *Dad's Army.* Beside Wentworth Stringer stood Rollo, who had certainly lost weight — so much so that Kelp had had to provide some braces to keep him decent now that his waistline had slimmed somewhat. Albert Blackhead still had a trilby planted firmly on his head as his trademark. His clothes had been soaked so many times that Kelp had had to produce a strange pair of green corduroy trousers and a sports jacket which had seen better days.

Wentworth Stringer had sent a messenger to Rosie offering her a lift to the Barracks from Government House, rather than put her in the position of having to travel to the Barracks with General Hernando. She accepted and came briskly out of a Government House still occupied by General Hernando and his staff, and got into the front passenger seat of the car. The Three Musketeers were crushed in the back. No-one attempted any small talk in the five minute journey to the Barracks. Wentworth

Stringer simply said, 'Here we are,' when they arrived and got out quickly so as to be able to open Rosie's door. Ever the gentleman, thought Rosie.

General Wallop marched up and saluted and shook hands with each MP in turn. He then indicated a row of chairs behind a single chair which was behind a table. On the opposite side of the table was a single chair.

Opposite the table across the square the Marranesian forces in olive green uniforms were drawn up. At either end of the square were Companies from the Scots Guards and a Company from the Parachute Regiment and a Company from the Welsh Guards. Behind the table a Company of Royal Marines was deployed, with the Royal Marine Band to one side of the table, back some thirty yards. All of the British units had distinguished themselves in various actions to retake the Islands.

At the precise appointed moment General Hernando and his immediate staff drove onto the Square. General Hernando, carrying his sword, marched smartly to the table and saluted General Wallop, who returned the salute. Both Generals then turned to face the flagpole in front of the Headquarters building. The Marranesian national anthem was played as the Marranesian flag was lowered and then *God Save the Queen* as the Union flag was raised in its place.

General Wallop then invited General Hernando to take his seat and staff officers placed the surrender documents in front of both Generals. Both copies had to be signed and then exchanged. The Generals stood and saluted. The media cameras flashed and popped. Army PR Officers were having a field day. General Hernando then presented his sword to General Wallop. The official humiliation of the Marranesians was complete. It was now time for General Hernando to go, but not until a proper lunch had been served.

★★★

Albert felt that he had waited his entire life for this moment, a moment when he could make his own preferences prevail and when he could even have a decisive influence on events. No more the bit player. For once Albert would be centre stage.

It was his innate sense of fair play that drove him. There was something seriously decent about Albert. He did need, however, a fellow conspirator. Someone who shared his sense of fair play and a detestation of injustice.

The British authorities were keen to play everything by the book. A handsome lunch of smoked salmon and cold chicken was produced and the two Generals and their staffs were seated to enjoy it. The MPs ate in an anteroom.

Conversation flowed at the military table, with or without interpreters. Theirs was the talk of military men after the battle. The physical challenge was over and the talking could begin. The British Commander was magnanimous and generous to his defeated opponent, despite any personal disinclination to be so. His Foreign Office brief had described Hernando as what would have been called in World War Two terms an SS General.

For his part, although Hernando was glad to be talked to about military matters, there was little that could be said to lift his sense of impending doom concerning his return to Marranesia. War failures were not welcome. The germ of an idea began to form in his mind.

The atmosphere at the MPs' table was altogether more subdued. Wentworth Stringer was thinking of Rosie. Rosie was thinking about Wentworth Stringer. Wenty wanted no personal vendetta, but somehow felt Rosie was getting away with it.

Rosie was consumed with guilt, felt that she was probably being cowardly in not returning to face the music and not at all optimistic about her future as a non-Spanish speaking widow in Marranesia — as Hernando had assured her she soon would be. Rosie had an idea.

Rollo was feeling post-adrenaline tiredness and a sense of anti-climax now it was all over. He was indifferent to Rosie's fate, regarding any punishment as nothing less than natural justice.

Albert was very quiet. He had become a cliché-free zone, for which the others gave thanks. Presently, Albert got up from the table and went outside.

The Military Commanders' lunch was concluding with photographs and handshakes. The Generals, trailed by their staff, walked to the reception area of the Barracks and met up with the MPs minus Albert, of whom there was no sight. Rosie had excused herself to the powder room and re-emerged some time later looking tired and over-made up.

It was now time to go. Hernando and Rosie said goodbye to everyone and were shown into a staff car for the journey to the airport. Hernando had surrendered his sword and pistol to the British but he had a small dagger hidden down the back of his right sock. His plan was to take over the plane and change the flight destination to one of Marranesia's neighbours where he could seek political asylum.

Rosie's plan was to get Hernando to drink a toast to their future and she had already laced the bottle with a powerful sleeping substance. She had to neutralise Hernando first and then try to bribe the crew to fly to one of Marranesia's neighbours. Rosie and Hernando had identical aims if only they had confided in each other.

The staff car arrived alongside the old business jet used by the Marranesian Air Force for VIP travel. The pair were greeted by a Sergeant of the Marranesian Air Force who saluted and conducted them to their seats. Rosie and the General sat opposite each other with pull-down tables for when it came to feeding time. The sergeant, with olive green forage cap well pulled down, ensured that their seatbelts were fastened and gave the safety spiel, including the one and a half hours' flying time to Gazebo, the Marranesian capital.

In response to the 'Can I get you anything before takeoff?' question, Rosie asked for two glasses. No need to hang about, she thought. The sooner he takes the potion, the better.

Rosie produced a bottle of local red wine from a large bag she had with her and quickly poured out two glasses.

'Here's to us!' said Rosie.

'Cheers!' said Hernando, drinking his wine and thinking what on earth was he going to do with this human reminder of his humiliation. Rosie managed to knock over her wine glass, almost too convincingly, so that a large red stain appeared on her skirt.

Presently the plane taxied to the runway and then with a sustained roar it took off towards the north east. The RAF Harrier pilot on combat air patrol at 10,000 feet saw the plane take off and noticed that it had not changed course, as would have been customary for anyone flying to Gazebo to the north west. He continued to watch the plane as it climbed to a cruising altitude.

The General was very alert when it came to landmarks and routes and he noticed at once that the plane appeared to be on a different course to the one he had expected. Whatever plans he had for the plane's eventual destination, the initial course should be towards Gazebo.

The General undid his seatbelt and stood up quickly. Rosie noted with satisfaction that he swayed on his feet and put a hand up to his head. The General held on to the back of the seat as the plane continued its climb.

The Sergeant glanced over his shoulder on the flight deck and saw the General on his feet. The General should not have undone his seatbelt, but a General is a General. The Sergeant said something to his co-pilot and then undid his own pilot's shoulder belts and turned to greet the General.

Rosie had her back to the flight deck, so she saw nothing of what followed. The Sergeant saluted the General and stood back with a gesture to allow the General to pass through the flight deck. Even if Rosie had not had her back to what happened next, she would have been hard-pressed to follow, so quickly did things happen.

As the General passed the Sergeant, the Sergeant took out a heavy-duty spanner and struck the General with it on the back of his head. The General crashed down, Rosie swung round, thinking this was the work of her magic potion, to find the Sergeant lifting the General and pulling him back into his seat. The Sergeant then did up the General's seatbelt and, to Rosie's amazement, clicked a pair of handcuffs onto the General. That operation having been performed, the Sergeant stood up and removed his cap.

'Pedro!' said Rosie. 'What are you doing here? I never knew you could fly', she added.

The Sergeant smiled. 'I am a man of many parts', he replied. 'I decided there were some home truths which the General needed to hear. I am sorry you are with him still. Why don't you go to the flight deck and meet my colleague? He is not a pilot but I have set a course on auto pilot.'

Rosie was intrigued. Things were going better than planned. The General was trussed up like a turkey and could be stuffed later by whichever authorities were interested. She would now step forward to the flight deck.

The pilot occupied the left hand seat. As Rosie got closer she became aware of something unusual about his appearance. She stared hard to make sure she could believe the evidence of her eyes. The 'pilot' was wearing a brown trilby hat with the earphones crammed down on top. It was Albert.

Rosie clutched the doorway for support. Her head swam. From a situation of high promise she was now faced with inexplicable collapse. Albert had never been good news. Albert represented well-meaning, muddled, patriotic Old Labour. Albert was not the person to be on the burning deck with or to be on a desert island with or to be anywhere with if your life depended on it. She reeled back towards her seat and collapsed into it.

Pedro then bent over and fastened her seatbelt. 'There now, Mrs Long. You should take it easy. There is no point in getting in a state.' Pedro was calm and very firm. Rosie looked flushed and furious.

'What are you doing, Pedro?' she asked. 'Why did you hit the General?'

'The General needs to be under control. He will come round soon. Then he will be made to face some truths.'

'What truths?'

'He will be shown photographs of people he tortured.'

'Members of your family?'

'My brother and our neighbour. They were only two of many, but they were special. I hoped the British would keep the General and put him on trial. Their Intelligence must know all about him but they seem to want to hand him back very quickly. I don't understand.'

Pedro sat across the aisle from Rosie and the unconscious General. He looked comfortable in his uniform and Rosie thought he was quite attractive. Certainly his eyes had an intensity about them which was startling, and which Rosie had never felt or noticed before.

Pedro looked at Rosie. 'You don't want to go to Marranesia, do you?' he asked quietly as though concerned that the General might wake up. Rosie could see no point in deception.

'No. I decided there was no future for me in Marranesia.

Hernando — the General — helped me to that conclusion. He told me that he would either be put on trial or he would have an accident quite soon and then I would be on my own. A British politician in a country with whom we have just fought a war and unable to speak the language. Not a good prospect for a widow.'

'So what's your plan, Mrs Long?'

'My main plan was to stop the General and me from going to Marranesia. As I didn't think he'd agree, I put a sleeping draught in his drink before take-off. I think he was already feeling the effects when you hit him on the head.'

'Where do you plan to end up, Mrs Long?' The questioning was polite, but persistent. The General slumbered and Albert clung to the controls as the plane droned on.

'I don't mind. Anywhere that is not Marranesia — and the UK, of course — and where we can be together.'

Pedro thought for a moment before the next question and then it was a statement.

'From certain things the General has said I don't get the impression that 'we' is an appropriate word to use.'

'What do you mean?' shot Rosie.

'The General is married. He could get his wife to join him in another country if that's where we go, Mrs Long. I am sorry to be brutal.'

Rosie paused and then said, 'You bastard.' As she said this she leaned over and whacked the recumbent General across the face as hard as she could. The General groaned. Rosie shook the General and smacked his face again. 'I want to talk to you! Wake up!'

Pedro bent down and undid the General's left boot and removed it. He then felt under the General's left trouser leg and presently removed a small, vicious-looking knife.

'I remembered he usually carried this,' said Pedro. 'I think he had a plan too. I don't think he likes the idea of Marranesia any more than you do. I think the knife was going to be used to persuade me to fly the plane to a neighbour of Marranesia and the General would apply for asylum. As simple as that.'

'And you, Pedro. What is your plan?' asked Rosie.

'I have told you', replied Pedro. 'I want to bring the General face to face with his past. It means a lot to me.'

'But you can't go back to Marranesia either?' queried Rosie.

'No', replied Pedro.

'Then where are you going?'

'Nowhere.'

'What do you mean 'nowhere'?'

'What I said. The General was coming to the flight deck because he had noticed from landmarks on the ground that we were not flying north west, as one would for Marranesia, but north east.'

'Where does north east lead us?'

'Precisely nowhere. We cannot make the next landfall because we won't have enough fuel. When we run out of fuel we crash in the sea. Death will be instantaneous.'

There was silence for a moment and then Rosie erupted.

'You're mad, you people, all mad! There's no need for us all to die.' She leapt to her feet and made for the flight deck. Pedro grabbed her and as she struggled frantically he wished that he had put the other pair of handcuffs on her as well as the General. She fought like a tigress. He held her as they fell to the floor of the aisle.

'Albert is the one who has plans for you, Mrs Long, but you'll have to talk about them through the door because I can't —' Pedro never finished the sentence because Rosie had launched another furious assault. She had managed to get a hand free and went straight for Pedro's genitals, firmly presented as they were in the army uniform. Rosie squeezed as hard as she could. Pedro was now totally co-operative and crashing on the floor. Rosie sprang past him onto the flight deck and slammed the door.

'Albert, is there any way I can lock this door? Pedro is mad.'

Albert turned slightly from his seat and indicated a push-in button to the left of the door. 'Push that', he said. Rosie pushed the button and the light changed from green to red. 'Only the General knows the code to open that door, so I hope he's awake — if we need him', said Albert.

Rosie decided that there was no need to apprise Albert of the General's condition. In any case, she had some questions to ask Albert now that Pedro was being sick on the other side of the flight deck door.

Rosie settled herself in the seat alongside Albert, who had

removed his trilby so that the headphones could fit snugly on his head. Albert stared ahead, holding course. All around him there was a vast emptiness of sky and sea. He loved it. Above all he loved the feeling of control.

'Albert', began Rosie, 'Why are we on a course to nowhere?' She tried to sound mildly curious rather than overwrought. After all, it was hardly an everyday occurrence for an aircraft to fly on a course which was suicidal providing the crew had not succumbed to loss of oxygen pressure. Rosie reflected for a second, but only for a second, that the crew of her aircraft had sufficient oxygen but had taken leave of their senses. It would all be the subject of a Parliamentary Enquiry, of course. When they got down. If they got down.

★★★

Back in the Control Tower at Port Roger there was consternation. Ever since the aircraft had failed to correct its course towards Marranesia after take-off and had continued on a north-easterly course, the alarm had gone up the military chain of command.

Wentworth Stringer and Rollo were having a post-prandial glass of whisky with the General when the news arrived.

Here was the Commander in Chief of the Marranesian invasion forces being flown the 400 miles to Gazebo, the Marranesian capital, and already the plane was seriously off course. The general consoled himself with the thought that General Hernando was at least being flown by his own people. But what on earth were they up to? Wentworth Stringer made a guess.

'I think General Hernando does not plan to go to Marranesia at all.'

'Fair enough', replied the General. 'But that still doesn't explain the course the plane's on. Group Captain, could they made landfall with the amount of fuel they've got?'

'No they couldn't, sir', asserted the Group Captain.

'Then I think we'd better turn them round back here, Group Captain. We have Harrier GR3s keeping tabs on the plane, I assume?'

'Yes, sir'.

★★★

At sixteen thousand feet Squadron Leader Ginger Swordblood had been keeping the Marranesian jet under surveillance. Now he was ordered to close in and deploy the standard procedures to indicate that the Marranesian aircraft was to follow him. He closed in and took up a position on the starboard wing of the Marranesian plane. On the flight deck he could see a man and a woman. They seemed to be having a very intense discussion; it might almost have been an argument. They certainly had no time to see him.

Back at Port Roger the British General decided to go to the Control Tower himself and this he did with his staff and with the two MPs.

By the time the group reached the first floor of the modest-sized Port Roger Control Tower, Squadron Leader Swordblood was coming alongside his quarry.

'Control, this is Red One. I am now abeam Marranesia 14 and I can see two people on the flight deck, a man and a woman. They are not looking out. Over.'

'Roger, Red One. Try and attract their attention if you can. We can't seem to raise them from here. Over.'

Squadron Leader Swordblood continued to fly abeam, to no avail. He decided he must do something different, so he pulled up and flew directly over the Marranesian plane and pulled across two hundred yards in front of it so that the crew should see him if they were aware of anything.

To his astonishment, no sign of recognition came from the Marranesian jet, no waggling of the wings or other internationally agreed signal. This was not too surprising in that neither of the two people on the flight deck had ever even sat in flight deck seats before, let alone flown any plane. The crew of the Marranesian jet had, however, seen the Harrier.

'My God, it's the RAF', said Albert. 'That's a Harrier. I wonder what he wants?'

They both stared as the plane returned to take up its position, so close that they could see the pilot's ginger moustache, and they started trying to decipher his hand signals. Albert decided that he should be properly dressed, so he put the trilby back on.

'Control, this is Red One. I now have their attention. They have not yet responded. I am trying to get them to turn and follow me. This may seem odd, Control, but the man has put on a trilby hat. Over.'

Wentworth Stringer sat bolt upright. Albert! No wonder they hadn't seen him anywhere since the ceremony. What on earth was going on? The woman on the flight deck was obviously Rosie, which meant that neither of them could fly the plane.

'General, I have an awful feeling that my two parliamentary colleagues are on the flight deck of that plane. Neither of them has the remotest idea how to fly, although I think Albert is trying things out.'

For the British General a potential diplomatic incident was turning into a nightmare with two MPs at risk.

Squadron Leader Swordblood looked at the passenger compartment and reported he thought he could see two people close together; one seemed to be standing over the other one.

Rosie worked it out first. 'He wants us to turn round,' she cried. 'We can go back to Port Roger'. There was a note of relief, almost triumph, in her voice. Then a note of uncertainty. 'Do you know how to turn round, Albert?'

'We did a turn after take-off. He called it banking, I think, although I couldn't see any money in it. It went like this.' Albert disengaged the auto pilot and then, with a very light touch, gently eased the controls to port and the plane began to respond. He had to make a note of the course setting because he would be flying back on what pilots call the reciprocal. In any case, he need only follow the Harrier, which was itself turning to take up its position abeam and slightly above.

'Albert, now that we are going back, you haven't given me a proper answer. Why were we flying on a course to oblivion?'

'Because there was nowhere else for us to go', Albert replied. 'Pedro and I had not planned anything. We were brought together to be instruments of the Hand of God.' Rosie was silent, taken aback once again on this extraordinary flight.

'Albert, are you all right?'

'Am I all right! That's typical of you, is that. What would someone from Barnsley be doing talking about the Hand of

God — and it wasn't Diego Maradona either! I know what you're thinking. That I'm stupid Old Labour, and you are the worst of all 'cos you're not even New Labour. You're stuck somewhere in between. Desperately trying to get across the pontoon bridge to get into the cocktail parties with all those luvvies. We Old Labour people are proud of who we are and where we come from and we mean no illwill to the New types, all these ones in suits who go out to lunches with businessmen. One day in the future these people will help to make us electable again. There's no sign of it yet, mind. With this Faraways War she's invincible, but every dog has its day. One day we'll be back and it'll be young men in suits and ties that'll do it. The likes of you won't help. You'll just ride like over-made up tick birds on the back of our great Party. You disgust me, you and your type! That wouldn't have been enough to invoke the Hand of God. It's this war that's done it. You were a traitor to our country. You broadcast for the enemy, an enemy who had used force on British citizens and fought our troops. You are as much a traitor as Lord Haw Haw or Mata Hari. As far as I was concerned there was no way you were going to fly off into the sunset like one of them movies with Ingrid Bergman and the other bloke. You are a traitor and you must be punished as a traitor. In 1918 you would have been shot. Today you will die in an aeroplane and I will see you do it because I am going to die with you to make sure.'

The only sound was of Rosie sobbing.

Albert pressed the R7 switch and spoke to Control in Port Roger.

'Hello, Control. This is the Marranesian VIP jet and this is Albert Blackhead. How far are we from you? Over.'

'Marranesian 14. This is Control. You are sixty miles north east of Port Roger. The wind here is from the south east at ten knots.'

Albert had been reading up a few things in the books and he knew that Control would give wind speed and direction because these were essential elements in the process of landing. Albert, however, had no intention of landing. It was nearly time for the display.

When Albert was interested in anything he was a good learner.

They always said that at his schools. He had been interested in flying for a long time, starting as a boy with Captain W E Johns and Biggles. He had graduated through Lindbergh and Amy Johnson to modern times and the Battle of Britain. He has since found through watching Pedro that all the manoeuvres he had read about could be reproduced. All he lacked, and it was a large deficiency, was the experience to carry them out.

In the Control Tower tension was as high as it could get. In a matter of minutes the VIP plane would appear somewhere near the airfield, if not directly overhead. They were now able to talk to the plane so they must have a good chance of talking the plane down.

As the two MPs comprised the flight deck, the British General asked Wentworth Stringer to be the interlocutor, the man who would talk his colleagues safely down.

'Control, this is Red One. He's approaching the airfield now, range fifteen miles.'

'Roger, Red One. Keep him observed', the Group Captain replied.

'Control, Red One. His angle of approach is too flat. It's as though he's trying to come in under the radar. I suggest you tell him to increase his height. Over.'

'Roger, Red One. Marranesia 14, you need more height for your approach. Over.' No reply.

'Marranesia 14, roger my last transmission. Over. ' No reply.

The plane was now nearly at the end of the runway and no more than a hundred feet in the air. It was now clear to everyone in the Control Tower that the plane was not making an approach to land. Indeed, it was positively averse to landing. It had no intention of landing. The plane roared across the airfield with all eyes staring in amazement.

Albert pulled back the stick. Rosie screamed. The plane climbed steeply and then banked suddenly to starboard. Albert eased the controls and began flying in a circle back to the far end of the airfield. Wentworth Stringer was on the Control tower radio.

'Albert, this is Wentworth. What are you doing? Over.' No reply.

The plane had now climbed to about four thousand feet and Albert was performing some manoeuvres gleaned from his handbook *Flying in Six Easy Lessons* by Amy Johnson, roaring back and forth across the airfield each time.

Wentworth Stringer knew he was onto a lost cause, but he tried again.

'Albert, this is Control. We can talk you down. We can tell you what to do. You don't have to worry about anything. Over.' No reply.

Suddenly Rosie's voice was there loud and firm and clear.

'You must help us. Everyone's mad on the plane. I want to live.'

The Control Tower heard the sound of the door to the cockpit being opened. General Hernando could be heard saying something in Spanish.

Pedro had taken off the General's handcuffs the better to let him see and handle the photographs of the disappeared. The General suddenly attacked Pedro by kicking him in his sensitive parts and then he reached for the keyboard and punched in the numbers which he alone knew in order to open the door to the flight deck.

Albert was aware of the General's arrival and immediately put the plane into a vertical climb. The General and Pedro slid down the aisle to the lavatory at the back. Rosie moaned and then began to sing *The Blaydon Races* in a soft voice.

Albert banked the plane, levelled out and turned towards the nearby mountain range.

Wentworth Stringer tried again. 'Albert, Albert. This is Wenty. Blue Fox. We need you here.'

'Bollocks'. It was Albert. No-one ever knew whether he was replying to Wentworth Stringer or commenting on the rapidly approaching mountain range.

The flash was seen before the sound of the impact was heard. The wreckage was scattered widely. Albert's hat and Rosie's prized and much-used make-up case were soon identified. General Hernando and Pedro appeared to be locked in an embrace. The Prime Minister was informed at once.

★★★

The military set a lot of store by decorum — doing things right even in difficult circumstances — preventing hats being blown off when helicopters lift off — that sort of thing. There was therefore widespread interest among the Task Force that the Prime Minister's C130 was due to travel through one of the worst storms forecast to hit the region.

There was additional malicious joy that the Chief of the Defence Staff himself, Sir Trimmer Halliard, had been unable to avoid making the trip to Port Roger. Nor had the Governor, Mr Cunningham, been forgotten. The Prime Minister insisted that he accompany her wearing his full regalia so that she could try to erase the memory of that humiliating picture of Rosie Long kissing the feet of the conquering General Hernando.

The Prime Minister's fury with Rosie Long and her getting killed with Albert Blackhead, and her mixed feelings about Arthur Mafeking's death in the hour of victory, were almost enough to keep her mind off the rocking and bucking of the C130 as it plunged into the clouds. All her staff were sick. The loo was in constant use. The RAF cabin staff were much too nervous to ask the Prime Minister if she was all right.

Eventually Port Roger came into view below and preparations were made for landing. The Prime Minister was looking decidedly pale. For Admiral Halliard it was no worse than a force 10 in the Atlantic. Governor Cunningham was concerned about keeping the creases in his white uniform in the right place. His cocked and plumed hat was in his hand.

The C130 made its final approach and touched down, then taxied to the control tower, where the Royal Marine Band and a Guard of Honour were drawn up. General Wallop and ADC could be seen waiting. All eyes on board were on the Prime Minister. Had she made it safely down or would the contact with very fresh Faraways air when the door opened be the *coup de grâce*?

Everything went well at first. The Prime Minister came down the steps and was saluted by General Wallop. Then it went wrong, but it went wrong with a precision that would have made the Brigade of Guards proud. The Prime Minister twirled round to Governor Cunningham and said one word to him.

'Hat,' she said.

He at once gave her his pride and joy and she at once was sick into it. The Prime Minister paused for a moment, then straightened up and dabbed her lips with a handkerchief from her cuff. She then hissed to Governor Cunningham, 'Put it on. I want that picture.' Decades of Foreign Office training paid off as Cunningham crammed the hat back on his head.

Once again a vomit-ridden situation at Port Roger airport was saved by Kelp. Kelp was on hand on the bank nearby and quick as a flash, while the Prime Minister was turning round to face General Wallop, Kelp emptied a bucket of water over Governor Cunningham and said, 'Welcome back, sir.'

The media were positioned on a platform some little distance off and had to use their zooms.

Prime Minister thanks victorious Governor and *Prime Minister is welcomed back by our Governor* would be the headlines. Few would know that Governor Cunningham's contorted grimace originated from something other than emotion at the Prime Minister's arrival on Faraway soil. Nonetheless, the plumes just managed to flutter and the photographic record was put straight.

The Prime Minister was now driven away to Government House to recover from the journey and to prepare for a dinner party which she was to host in honour of General Wallop.

The dinner party itself was a friendly and informal affair. The Prime Minister was hosting Admiral Sir Trimmer Halliard, Governor Cunningham, General Wallop and his main military subordinate commanders and chief of staff, the two MPs, Kelp, in view of his heroic role in the campaign, and John Mulch in recognition of his role and also representing the Islands community. The whole enterprise of retaking the Islands had been considerable. The atmosphere now was a mixture of relief and exhilaration.

The Prime Minister proposed a toast, thanking all present for their wonderful efforts and closing with the lines from Henry V.

John Mulch had been persuaded — with some difficulty because he was completely overawed by the Prime Minister — to speak in response for the Islands and their people and give thanks for their deliverance. He spoke simply and highly effectively.

There was to be no victory parade in Port Roger. The focus would be on the funerals of Lord Mafeking, Rosie Long, Albert Blackhead and Sergeant Pedro. A Marranesian plane had arrived and taken the coffin of General Hernando to Gazebo.

The everlasting Faraways wind was blowing strongly as the Prime Minister arrived at ten o'clock at the Church of St Mungo, a small tin-roofed church with a worshipping congregation of about fifty most Sundays, and about three times that number on the High Days. There was some ill-feeling that not all the regulars could be accommodated, but with the large number of dignitaries to be fitted in, the church was too small for the occasion. The Royal Engineers had arranged for the service to be relayed to Port Roger Secondary School and the overflow was taken care of in that way. The coffins had been placed on gun carriages draped in the union flag. On Lord Mafeking's coffin were his decorations and a hearing aid. On Albert's coffin was a brown trilby hat and on Rosie Long's coffin a make-up brush and a masonic trowel. Sergeant Pedro had nothing on his coffin.

The Royal Marines Band would lift any occasion, thought the Prime Minister, as she and Chief of Defence Staff, the Governor and General Wallop and John Mulch sat in the front pew. Even so, the Royal Marines buglers were hard-pressed to be heard above the noise of hailstones falling on the tin roof.

The Rector of Port Roger gave rather a good, if over long, sermon. It was, after all, a moment of glory which he had never expected to have. The Prime Minister found herself drifting into her own thoughts. What an extraordinary turn of events this was! By virtue of a freak accident, the British people had been provided with the combination that they most fervently seek — victory and a hero. Victory they demanded and expected in war, football, cricket and any lesser sport where foreigners are suspected of practising beforehand and cheating on the day. Heroes such as Monty, Bobby Charlton and Ian Botham achieved cult status until the books began to appear accusing them of homosexuality or stealing from their mothers.

In the death of Lord Mafeking the British were taken right back to Nelson. No matter that Mafeking's demise was somewhat more mundane than Nelson's, nor that the threat to England in 1805 was somewhat more serious than the loss of the Faraways, the media already had the story they wanted. Lady Mafeking was too upset to attend the funeral and interment, but there would be a memorial service in London later. Lord Mafeking's family history was researched exhaustively. Numerous facts that no-one could possibly want or need to know were produced. Some items, like Lord Mafeking's appalling grades at Eton, were edited out as unsuitable for a heroic encomium, but to be held back for the iconoclastic backlash in a few years' time.

I knew dunderhead Mafeking at school type of thing.

What had seemed to be an opportunity to give thanks for victory and deliverance and to express gratitude for an unlikely war hero had now taken on a touch of almost Greek tragedy, with three more coffins accompanying that of his Lordship. Even in death Lord Mafeking was to be flanked by people whom he despised and never understood.

The media now had everything. If they struggled to make Lord Mafeking their hero, they struggled even harder to make Albert Blackhead their star. The stories were, however, being written of his daredevil wizardry at the controls of the plane and his exploits with Blue Fox.

Rosie Long was another case altogether. She would repay further study to ask the questions and try to unravel a complex person. For now she was *Modern Mata Hari in Plane Crash Horror!*

Wentworth Stringer found himself being saluted smartly by an Army Sergeant as he left Government House. 'Sergeant Banger, sir. I have been sent to take you to the funeral.'

Wentworth Stringer allowed himself to be propelled into the back of the car for the journey to St Mungo's.

As they set off, Sergeant Banger said cheerily, 'I think the Prime Minister has got some good news for you, sir.'

'Oh, really. What could that be, I wonder?'

After the service the Prime Minister sought out Wentworth Stringer and said, 'Wenty, dear. I want you to be Deputy Chief Whip. It's all arranged. Welcome to the Government. Your driver will find you outside.' She patted his forearm affectionately. The Prime Minister quite liked military men — in small doses.

Outside the Church Sergeant Banger was quickly at Wentworth Stringer's side. 'I believe congratulations are in order, sir.'

Wenty was taken aback. 'Why yes, thank you.'

Once inside the car Wentworth Stringer found an envelope on the seat. It was addressed to him. He opened it. It was headed *Draft evidence to the House of Commons Defence Select Committee.* 'Who is this from?'

'Should we say I arranged it, sir, in case you might need it on your return.'

Wentworth Stringer shook his head. 'Extraordinary fellow', he said to himself.

Some time later, after the burial in the cemetery overlooking Port Roger, the media gathered for more photographs and to look at the messages on the wreaths. One reporter found a touching message from a member of the Task Force, which said:

In Memory of Lord Mafeking

Who stood up for freedom but forgot to look first

It was signed: John Banger. Sergeant.